OBaaT

a novel by

ALICE VACHSS

Pay What it Costs
Publishing, LLC

Library of Congress Control Number: 2024921137

Publisher's Cataloging-in-Publication Data

Names: Vachss, Alice, author.
Title: OBaaT / Alice Vachss.
Description: South Beach, OR:
Pay What it Costs Publishing, LLC, 2025.
Identifiers: LCCN: 2024921137 |
ISBN: 978-0-9968554-4-0 (paperback) |
978-0-9968554-3-3 (ebook)

Subjects: LCSH Friendship--Fiction. |
Bullying--Fiction.| Schools--Fiction. | Child
abuse--Fiction. | Foster home care--Fiction. | BISAC
YOUNG ADULT FICTION / Social Themes / Activism
& Social Justice | YOUNG ADULT FICTION / Social
Themes / Bullying | YOUNG ADULT FICTION /
Social Themes / Friendship
Classification: LCC PS3622 .A34 O33 2025 | DDC 813.6--dc23

Manufactured in the United States of America
First Edition

Credits
Front Cover and Photo:
Andrew Vachss https://www.vachss.com
Cover and Book Design:
Darlene K Swanson https://van-garde.com/
Pay What it Costs logo:
Geof Darrow https://www.facebook.com/geofdarrow

for my true love

Sad would come later, right after angry. But for now I was happy. I'd stayed true. That's who I am. The people who love me will be proud. The rest—I won't care.

. . .

Mrs. Harbinger had been apologetic: "I'm sorry Anna. I made a mistake." I wondered if she meant saying "yes" when I'd first asked, or saying "no" now. I thought to myself: *I get it. Teachers have bosses. But we all believed you were different. Better.*

It had started in the girls bathroom. Our lovely Piper in tears, her perfect makeup streaking down her face. Lance had scared her . . . again. We heard him outside the door. Three knocks, then three again, then four. Piper had told us once it was his code for "you are mine." Soft, sweet-hearted Sunny abandoned a failed attempt to hug Piper's hurt away. Lots of us are angry, but Sunny . . . we didn't expect her to be the one out of all of us who'd had enough: "I'm tired of this. All of it. I don't know why I thought people would be different now. Or why I thought junior year would be better. But even though everything changed, nothing's changed. Yesterday Mr. Beemer made Ethan cry in class. Last week that new girl, she came back from the weekend more black and blue than she was on Friday. And I know something's wrong with you, Jade, but you won't tell any of us what it is."

We all held our breath, but Jade only looked down at the floor. Except for a heated red flush, you couldn't tell she'd even heard. I *had* to say something to take the spotlight off her. That's when I came up with the idea. We'd start an I-Hate-Bullies campaign right here at the school. A million possibilities—I now think are weak—popped out in a rush: Instas. Artwork. Poems. The list kept getting longer. Anybody could join us.

Mrs. Harbinger let us announce it in our creative writing class. More people signed up than I expected but that was in front of their friends. We'd see who really showed up for the first meeting.

That was in third period. Just before the final bell I got a message to report to the language arts classroom. Even while Mrs. Harbinger was saying her don't-blame-me words like "administration" and "going through channels," it was obvious I was going to hear some final, permanent "not happening."

I'm no techie. I got some help. Now there's a Facebook page called OBaaT. It stands for One Bully at a Time. I was going to go the good-girl route but they wouldn't let me. Their rules prohibited it. Now, there's no rules.

By the time I walked into the Boring Brick Building the next morning, word had gotten out. Everyone just assumed I-Hate-Bullies was a non-starter. Idiots.

Time for trusted friends only. After school. At Dareen's, of course.

Dareen's family lives in an apartment above her mother's impossibly busy walk-in medical clinic. I think it's for women only; at least that's who stands in line out front. As long as we show up with book bulges in our backpacks and keep the noise level down, we have the whole upstairs to ourselves.

I started: "You all know we don't have 'official permission.' I won't blame any of you if you want to stop now," thinking: *I hope I'm not lying.* "But for me, this isn't over." I told them about OBaaT.

Dareen spoke first: "I'm in." Dareen can look like the meekest of us—she's got that downcast-eyes thing perfected whenever she wants it—but we all know better than that.

Piper's face reflected a million questions. *No one gets bullied here, Piper.* "I don't want to start with a bully we know." I guess she was worried we'd pick her boyfriend Lance. Beside her, Jade exhaled in relief that this wouldn't be a sideways attempt to help her either.

I'd had to learn that, too: Find how to fight for someone else before you can fight for yourself.

Even though her calling out Jade yesterday had started me on this path, today Sunny added her softness: "How harsh will we have to be?"

Tia—our parliamentarian—answered, "Group decision." She said it matter-of-fact, with that elegant calm that makes us all defer to her, but she looked a question at me. I nodded.

Tia gave OBaaT its first poem:

> Red danger,
> black terror,
> yellow caution,
> blue sadness ...
> what are the colors of kindness and
> courage?

We murmured our appreciation.

I'd been amazed that Rae-Rae had stayed quiet that long. Now she started to hum. It took us a while to recognize it—she'd taught us so much music we'd never heard before. Then we all joined in singing Martha and the Vandellas: "Dancing in the Street."

OBaaT. So, next we had to pick our first bully.

Tia called to semi-order our second meeting asking for candidate nominations.

Rae-Rae started us off confused when she bounced in singing, "For you, the living, this mash was meant too."

When our faces stayed puzzled she conceded, "OK you're right. Nobody remembers Bobby Pickett except around Halloween. And the 'Monster Mash' isn't really about mashing monsters—it's about monsters mashing!—but I liked the sound of it.

"Anyway, I've found my bully. Go with what you know, right? I've been checking out the locals, you know, music-wise. Who's more obvious to pick on than someone with big dreams? I found this guy. Besides sliming girls, he's lousy to his own band. So wrong. His music is definitely mediocre. The rest of the band are way better but he steps all over them. You can see they know it but they're like afraid of him. OK, maybe that last part is only in my head but I want to find out."

Tia suggested we each name our pick before we discussed them all.

Piper went next. Except when she's preoccupied with Lance, Piper kind of mocks herself about how focused she is on appearance. "I think our first OBaaT should look the part. You know, all fat and thug, sweats too much, bad teeth, major creep factor. I know, I know. Plenty of bullies don't look like that but for our first, someone uhggly would make a real impression. I scouted a coach, and that assistant to the guy who runs the Youth Ministry, and there's a 'food service specialist' I wouldn't want to be on her bad side—although the other lunch ladies are really sweet. But first, tell me what you think of going for the visual?"

Tia cut us off before we could answer by asking Dareen for a candidate.

"No one we know, right? Because I really want to pick my sister." She said it loud, as if she was hoping her sister was in their apartment within earshot.

"Maybe later," I said, trying to telepath a promise to her. I couldn't tell if she heard it.

Dareen shrugged it off: "You know that teacher who makes Ethan cry? I heard there's another kid in Ethan's class who always jumps in to sneer at Ethan as soon as Mr. Beemer says anything vicious. And then other kids follow. It makes me sick. It'd be easier if any of us were in that class but maybe we don't have to be to do something about it."

Tia warned, "Dareen—"

"—I got it," Dareen cut off the lecture. "Putting some pain on them would be . . . satisfying. But not what you all signed on for."

Tia sighed and then softened her voice to ask, "Jade?"

"Look, you all think you know something about me, but I'm not in this about me. That's not the rules, right? So yeah, I have a pick. And no, it's not personal. It's about that new girl. Who's bruising her up? Or is she hurting herself? I mean how skinny she is, that's not normal, right? And why isn't the school doing anything about it?"

Sunny agreed. "She was my pick too! It feels like if we ignore her hurt, we're part of what's hurting her." True Sunny, a tear rolled down her cheek.

"Anna?" Tia called on me.

"When I asked my techie to set up our page—"

"—Your secret techie—" Rae-Rae teased.

"—Secret is right!" I said defensively. "And he'll keep our secrets." Sunny patted the air and I dialed it back, remembering these were my friends I was talking to. "Look, if you want to, I'll ask him to be part of us. But I didn't know how comfortable you'd all be with a guy joining us. And if he's not with us then he's mine, not ours, OK?"

They all nodded without speaking so I continued: "What I was thinking is, he could find us someone who's being bullied online. He said it's an easy hack. Like on Snapchat, if someone deactivates an account, it stays alive for 30 days. It's simple, he says, to check which ones were taken down to stop online bullying, then work backward to find who was doing the cruel. Then when we trace that bully to his next victim, we dominate—"

Sunny interrupted: "Yeah, we could be all positive. We say we love her and admire her. The people screeching are the stupid ones, like that."

I sighed but let it go at that for now. "Tia," I said, "you don't get to just do spokesmodel here. Who's yours?"

"I don't know yet," Tia admitted. "Or maybe I do. You know the principal. Everyone calls him The Tsar for a reason. He hates us. Like he takes it personal when we don't suck up."

"Wow!" we all said before Tia backed off, saying that maybe that was breaking our first rule.

She ended the discussion with another of her poems:

> All good girls fear
>
> monsters under the murky.
>
> Even afraid, we fight.

A lot for now.

Rae-Rae got us past ourselves, bad-accent singing: "It caught on in a flash. It's now the mash. It's now the monster mash."

4

I held my breath when I walked into our talk-it-out meeting. My family—my only and true family—are my friends. I figure I can stand up to anything. Except I can't stand it when we argue. Anybody else, but not my friends. Tia knows this about me. It's why she takes charge of our serious discussions. Besides, that's Tia: serious.

I wasn't the only one worried. OBaaT had already become way scarier than when we had signed on.

Sunny only packed bite-sized Snickers for celebrations or peacemaking. "It's the perfect sneak snack food," she once insisted, "pre-wrapped and everything! I'm sure they would have called them 'Sneakers' if that wasn't already taken."

Dareen's family's rule was "No food during study group." Dareen had explained that the rule was about "concentration not nutrition."

Rae-Rae's envious response had been, "At least your rules are logical."

Usually we were good about the no-food prohibition. When we weren't, we CSI'ed the living room afterward. Despite Sunny's theory, there was a risk of Snickers smears. Today, before we began, Sunny quietly dispensed side hugs and chocolate.

Tia wanted to start us off. Of course. But Rae-Rae interrupted: "We've been talking." She gestured to no one in particular. We always keep private conversations private. "All our ideas are good but, like, later."

I looked her a question until Piper laughed: "Oh Rae-Rae, no one's going to get it without one of your songs."

All Rae-Rae needed was four syllables: "Yakety Yak!"

We all shouted/sang: "Don't talk back!" Sometimes The Coasters are exactly what we need.

"What Rae-Rae means," Piper continued, "is that all of our ideas are good but most of them can wait. The two that can't, I guess we think those are the new girl and Ethan."

Jade and Sunny looked relieved that we'd included the new girl. The rest of us nodded. That made sense. Rae-Rae gave us a tah-dah pose.

And now that I thought it was safe to, I volunteered, "I vote we start with Ethan—"

"—But first we ask him," Jade modified.

It didn't work out that way.

5

An announcement called the new girl out of class the next afternoon. When she hadn't returned by the end of last period, we knew. We all quietly assembled outside the ominously closed doors to the administrative offices.

I'd texted for permission on my safe phone, hoping I'd get an answer before I needed it. We had to wait another hour while the school emptied out. Halfway through I got a ping and read with relief the text that said, "Go for it. Stop by for a replacement."

Then I got permission from my friends.

When the doors finally opened, the new girl was sandwiched between a thickset woman and a wrinkled-suited man. Both of them looked angry, but not at the new girl. She simply looked worn down. Not sad or afraid. Just empty.

I stepped up but the adults tried to walk around me. My friends closed the gap enough to give me a minute. I handed the safe phone with its charger case to the new girl.

"I'm Anna," I told her. "I've been where you are. These are my friends. All of our numbers are in the phone. You can call or text us." I felt my friends nodding, standing with me. "The top number, that's my law guardian. She's a lawyer. She'll be your safety net if you don't like whoever they assign to you."

I wasn't sure the new girl understood what I said but she took the phone. The guy with the suit, his eyes had softened while I spoke to her. I hoped he'd explain better than I had.

After they left, Rae-Rae hummed sadly. We recognized it. Dionne Warwick: "Anyone who had a heart." Whoever was hurting the new girl, they didn't.

6

I always take one of my friends with me when I see my lawyer. Well, since I've *had* friends. This time it was Dareen. To protect my privacy but satisfy her grandmother, we needed a reason. We only had to stretch the truth a little: "a field trip to learn more about how the courts work." The part of town with all lawyers' offices is side-by-side with the courthouses, so it wasn't totally a lie.

When it's Dareen I bring with me, my lawyer always tries to talk up trial work as another way to do battle. Dareen's physical. They talked martial arts a lot this time and I pretended to be interested. I thought about my lawyer's face. How I knew it wasn't beautiful, but it was to me.

Dareen startled me back into the conversation: "Aren't you going to tell Naomi about OBaaT?"

Dareen calls my lawyer by her first name but I'm not comfortable doing that. The problem is I've never figured out how to say her name so I just sort of mumble something between Miss, Ms., and Mrs. In court, they call her all of those different things and she never corrects anyone. I'd say "Naomi Horne" but that sounds even more awkward so I skip using her name as much as I can.

I recited for my lawyer the condensed version of how I wound up giving away my safe phone. Ms. Horne replaced it. I immediately keyed in all my friends' phone numbers and then I felt better.

"We haven't heard from the new girl," I finished.

"You know I can't tell you if *I* have," my lawyer answered. I like it that she keeps everything confidential.

Dareen and Ms. Horne wanted to talk more about OBaaT. "Naomi's right," Dareen said. "If we're really all in with OBaaT, we need to have a meeting about safety, self-defense."

"But we're not talking about beat-kids-up-for-lunch-money bullies." I wanted to make sure they understood.

"I respect that," Ms. Horne told me solemnly. "But I think it's important to recognize that taking on people who abuse power could be dangerous. It only makes sense to be prepared."

"I'll tell Tia," I answered. I guess that was me agreeing to it.

Ms. Horne asked me about the Good Farmers. She knows that's what I call my foster couple. They're not abusers but they aren't . . . well, they *are* like good farmers: treat the livestock cruelty-free and benefit from a better payday. We're only product to them. Like when they want to go on vacation they send us back to a group home. The agency is not supposed to allow that. But it knows that if it refuses, then our foster couple will just return us all—like something they mistakenly purchased—and get replacements when they come back from wherever. The times I stay at a group home, I hear bad stories so I'm not complaining. But the foster couple, I never call them 'parents.'

"Same, same," I said. It's not that I don't like Ms. Horne. I think I admire her more than anybody. But I get quiet around her. I don't want her disappointed in me.

OBaaT planning meeting at Dareen's.

Rae-Rae walked in holding sheet music. "Nobody can sing Patsy but Patsy," she said. "Cline," she added, as if she hadn't told us about Patsy Cline a million times. Even without music, the lyrics made me sad: "I'm crazy for trying and crazy for crying."

We let Sunny be the one to ask because it would come out the sweetest from her: "Rae-Rae, what's going on?"

"The new girl texted me. She's homesick without a home." Rae-Rae half-smiled at the way she'd said it. We knew what she was thinking. She'd taught us a really silly song by Clarence 'Frogman' Henry.

We croak-sang the refrain to cheer her up: "I'm a lonely frog, I ain't got no home."

"Did she tell you her name, Rae-Rae?" I questioned her.

"Yeah. Charity Browne, B R O W N E. Why?"

"Do me a favor, then?" I asked. "Explain the emergency app to her. How she can send out an SOS to all the contacts on her safe phone at once. I didn't before because without a name what could we do about an SOS?"

Rae-Rae nodded. Because she still looked solemn Piper teased, "Why'd she choose you, Rae-Rae?"

It got a small but genuine smile. "Hey, if you were going to pick out a name from a list, would you go with one of the Plain Jane ones? Or would you figure that anyone called Rae-Rae would be the best?"

"You promised to be her friend, didn't you?" Sunny asked, approving.

"Hell, I promised we *all* would!"

Tia figured that was a good time to redirect the conversation. "Dareen?"

"OK," Dareen responded, all businesslike. "Naomi"— *Everybody knows my lawyer's name*, I thought proudly—"thinks OBaaT should have a session about self-defense. I asked my . . . I asked at the studio I train in and my teacher thinks he knows the correct person to talk to us. He'll arrange it if we want."

Dareen tries not to use words like 'sensei' and 'dojo' because the rest of us get confused trying to speak the language we don't ever get quite right. All of us, we speak different languages. The only one we've all needed to learn is Rae-Rae's because music is pretty much all she knows how to speak.

Everyone agreed to the meet-up. Sunny didn't ask why we needed self-defense although we all had expected that, being the most peaceable of all of us, she would.

Next on Tia's agenda: "Anna?"

"I haven't talked to Ethan yet," I admitted. "I guess I don't know what to say to him. I don't want him feeling . . . ganged up on, you know?"

"Maybe we can simply tell him we're worried about him?" Tia suggested.

"Nobody likes that!" Jade objected. *Message heard Jade, we're waiting on you to tell us what's wrong when you're ready.*

"Why not just spend some time with him and see if he shares anything?" Tia again.

"Yeah," I acknowledged. "There's some lecture he's all excited about that he wants me to go to with him."

Sunny cut short the conversation although it had mostly ended anyway. "I have to tell you something, guys."

Not at all like sweet Sunny. We all got quieter than we'd been.

"My mom and dad told me I should quit OBaaT. They think we're getting in over our heads."

What I've been waiting for. I tried to numb the pain before it hit too hard. "We understand—" I started, sorry I was less successful at sounding neutral than I intended.

"—Oh my god, no you don't!" Sunny interrupted. "I told them NO. This is too important."

I almost never cry but I must have looked like I was about to because Sunny gave me one of her biggest hugs. I didn't even try to duck out of it.

Piper didn't wait for Rae-Rae to start. Lesley Gore: "You don't own me."

Sunny joined in singing: "Don't tell me what to do. And don't tell me what to say." Then she qualified the lyrics with her own thoughts: "Still, I get it. I think they're right that we should be thoughtful about all this. Not just barge ahead."

We nodded. It's hard for me to remember that Sunny and her parents actually listen to each other. It doesn't fit anything I know.

"Anybody else?" Tia asked and we all shook our heads. I guessed there were no poems at a planning meeting

8

The studio looked like the cleanest, most symmetrical gym I'd ever been in. At the front of it sat a small black man, within himself. I don't think I ever understood the word "respectable" before. Like, worthy of respect. I tried to imagine what we must look like to him.

He knew Dareen, of course. To me what is striking is that she seems so self-contained but Dareen is most proud that her looks are what she calls "Habibati." She does have those dramatic eyes, that prow-of-a-boat strong-nosed profile, and thick, dark hair . . . but she says the hashtag is really about women redefining Middle Eastern beauty for themselves. That day in the studio, Dareen was standing a little differently than usual, as if she was center-balanced on the balls of her feet.

So was Tia. She's taller than Dareen and wears her hair very differently—blunt cut short and straight. Tia has that perfect maple syrup–colored skin that probably everyone would have if, well, the human race had more sense. Usually she reminds me of a pillar but her posture in the studio mimicked Dareen's. The small man gave her a slight nod. *She must train here too.*

Piper was the only one wearing make-up, pretty clothes, wavy hair curled just right. I don't know why she bothers because she's always that gorgeous kind of willowy. She could be Popular Girl so easily if that's what she wanted. Except for Lance, she mostly makes better choices.

Rae-Rae looks exactly like who she is. Masses of bouncy color-of-the-day curls and a whole bunch of energy in a skinny body. She always makes me think of a chrysanthemum.

Sunny never reminds me of a flower although she's a pouffy kind of blond. If the Pillsbury Doughboy were a teenage girl, he'd look like Sunny. I don't mean fat. Soft and floury and comforting. I'd never say it out loud but in my head, I always think of her as Sweet Sunny.

I didn't want to think about how Jade looked. Like she had an impenetrable force field around her. Jade once told us the gemstone she was named for could either be soft or hard. I didn't think, though, that it was meant to be brittle. She was always angular but before it had looked dramatic, like modern architecture. Everything about her used to be arty, expressive. Somehow the angles had sharpened. Standing in the studio, they looked painful.

And then there's me. I never know what I look like to other people.

Following my eyes enough to read my thoughts, Rae-Rae whispered: "It's true. If we were a girl group, if it hasn't already been taken, we'd have to call ourselves 'The Outcasts.' "

I looked over at the small man. I thought I saw the briefest crinkle to his eyes but it might only have been that I wanted to see it. He waited silently until we'd naturally settled into attention. When he eventually rose and spoke, there was something formal about the way he addressed us that made us know not to interrupt.

"Dareen has told me about OBaaT." He nodded at us with dignified approval. "I agree you need skills to protect yourselves from danger. Most such skills require years of investment. If those of you I do not know wish to be taken on as students, you are invited to do so."

Dareen and Tia stood taller. *That must be a great honor.*

"But for now, you need situational techniques you can readily learn. One of my best students knows you and he has been told of your intentions. He is waiting in the next room if you choose to be instructed by him. You may use that room now and whenever Dareen requests it on your behalf to conduct your OBaaT business. It is quiet and you will not be disturbed."

Arms at his sides and his motion flowing from the last of his words, he actually bowed from the waist to all of us at the end of his speech.

. . .

In the room assigned to us, the floor was so covered in mats that it took concentration to walk properly. In the center of the room was a stack of more mats, piled taller than any of us. Scattered around the stack was a random assortment of towels, pillows, and smaller mats. Between the teacher's words in our thoughts and the effort it required not to stumble, we were so preoccupied that it took us a moment to absorb who was waiting for us, seated cross-legged in one corner.

Ethan!

We worked really hard at controlling our faces. Tia said, as neutrally as only she could, "I did not know you were also a student here." She sounded formal like her teacher when she said it.

While he'd been waiting, Ethan must have been thinking about what to say to us because when he stood up, instead of answering Tia, he got straight to business: "The first task is to define the goal."

Something about the way he said that and Tia's and Dareen's silent amens feels . . . religious.

"You as a group have an honorable goal. Intrinsic in that goal is protection of the individuals in the group and it is the group itself that has the greatest power to do so."

Ethan always uses words I don't understand but if I'm patient he explains them.

"This is important. I am not here to teach you self-defense. How you walk down the street at night is not on the agenda. But if you as a group are going to take on bullies then you as a group may well face situations of physical danger. There are techniques to use your combined strength to mitigate that danger. I will teach you one."

He paused to see if we were following. Some yes, some—including me—not so much. I volunteered, "Maybe it will help if you show us, Ethan."

"Yes," Tia said, "but first can I add something here?"

Trust our parliamentarian to ask permission. I thought about it being Ethan who had come up with that title for Tia. Not that he'd known who I'd meant when I'd told him, "One of my friends, she always makes sure everyone gets a say, and everyone listens."

When he answered, "Oh, a parliamentarian," I looked it up but it didn't seem to fit.

"Why do you think that means she knows a lot about parliament?"

He explained—Ethan answers my questions without being judgy about me asking—"It's also come to mean someone who respects the fairness of rules and order."

Yes, that's Tia.

Now Tia was explaining Ethan's words: "People think the martial arts, they're like comic book hero stuff. They don't understand it's about something quiet inside yourself."

She didn't say the word "discipline" but I know that's what she meant.

Dareen jumped in: "I'm more about the combat than Tia, but I don't study to learn how to fight. I study in order to control my fighting instincts, not let them control me."

Rae-Rae summed it up: "So you're all saying, 'No Bruce Lee.'"

Whew.

"Exactly Rae-Rae!" Dareen answered and then handed back control of the conversation to Ethan by explaining: "Do you know in those movies the really stupid part where Bruce Lee is surrounded by enemies and he gets to defeat them one by one? If they all jumped in together—"

"—a less skilled or unskilled group can defeat any one individual," Ethan finished. "One more point before I take your suggestion, Anna. It is important to understand that your goal is not to *defeat* Bruce Lee. It is to *contain* him."

"Is this Bruce?" Rae-Rae asked, pointing to the stack of mats.

"Yes." Ethan smiled at her. "I don't want to teach you bad habits and I'm afraid that's what you'd get from one of those padded pretend villains who mock-threat in 'self-defense' classes. Besides"—he relaxed a little for the first time since we'd all walked into the room—"I don't want to *be* a padded-up villain."

Ethan seemed to appreciate it when Rae-Rae laughed.

"Here's how the exercise goes," Ethan continued. "Your job is to immobilize Bruce here. You might think that's easy because he's already, well, immobile. But the principles are the same. When I yell 'Threat!' you grab whatever is at hand. Your jacket, a towel or pillow, anything that can help wrap up Bruce and contain him. Then you simultaneously jump him."

The first time we tried it was just a mess.

"You are all too self-conscious," Ethan observed. "Tia and Dareen, you are trying to use too much skill. The rest of you, you are too worried about hurting each other. Again. Threat!"

By the fifth time, we were jumping in more or less at the same time. By the tenth time, we managed to topple the stack a little. After a while, Ethan singled each of us out one by one to, as he put it, 'get a visual' observing the others along with him. He kept us at it until we were sore and exhausted and starting to giggle instead of taking it seriously enough. Ethan read the room and called a break.

. . .

Most of us were friends with Ethan but individually, not together. Ethan was the first person at school who was ever nice to me. For a long time, he was the only one. Maybe that made us the closest. *I should speak up.*

"Ethan, I get it that we're learning to defend the group, but haven't you studied, like, self-defense?"

*Is there anyone in the room who doesn't know where this is go-
ing? Maybe Ethan.*

"Yes," he answered slowly. "I've always been big therefore you
wouldn't think I'd need to. But somehow I am a . . . target. I don't
want to be hurt and I've never wanted to hurt anyone. Studying my
discipline helped me learn how to accomplish both of those goals
at once."

Me again: "So you don't get hurt?"

"I don't get beaten up. Why are you asking this, Anna? . . .
Oh!" He inhaled sharply, studying all of our faces. "I'm someone
OBaaT wants to protect, aren't I?!"

Please, please, please. Don't be insulted, Ethan.

It wasn't until—after an achingly long pause—Ethan spoke
softly, "Thank you," that I started to breathe again.

"I don't fit in. Really I never have." Ethan could tell from
looking at us that we all understood what that felt like. "I am
emotional, which makes people uncomfortable. Some of their
reactions are ignorant, like calling me 'emo' even though I'm not
Goth or calling me gay—as if gay people are more emotional
than others." *Don't look at Tia. Hers to tell.* "And I'm intellectual.
They seem to think that's offensive too.

"But what hurts me is not that they don't like me, but their
intent. I don't know how to explain it." He gathered his thoughts
then tried again: "Cruelty makes me inexpressibly sad. That
people would act that way to each other. That it's part of the human character. I don't seem able to keep that feeling of sadness
to myself."

I didn't want Ethan to think he had to open himself up like
this. OBaaT was supposed to be about bullies. My lawyer had
taught me: " 'Victim' is a status, not a personality."

"Ethan, we heard there's one kid who—"

"—backs up every piece of hatred Beemer emits? Yes, Anna, there are several of them. Sycophants. They are not the root problem though."

A few of us looked confused at the word. "Suck-ups. Toadies. Parasites," Jade translated. It was the first thing she'd said all day. It sounded angry.

"Right," Ethan acknowledged, "and they are interchangeable. Interdict one and others will take his place. No, it is Beemer himself who is the problem."

I'd been listening intently when my lawyer and Sunny had discussed the role of bystanders a few months back. I wasn't sure I agreed with Ethan but I thought it was his call to make. Then he made it personal.

"Bullying by teachers, that is all kinds of abuse of power. Why do you think he stopped you Anna, when you tried to create the I-Hate-Bullies campaign?"

"It was Beemer who did that?" I asked in a smaller voice than I'd meant to.

"Yes, Anna. I know you blame Mrs. Harbinger—and she *was* wrong—but she was trying to soften the blow when she chose to be the one to tell you. Beemer went running to The Tsar as soon as he heard. The Principal and The Bully, they organized all the other autocrats and, well, you know the rest."

"We take on all the autocrats?" Dareen asked, hopeful.

"I wouldn't," Ethan answered. "I think if we can find a way for Beemer to face consequences, that would be a compelling message to all of them."

"I think you're very brave," Sunny whispered. She looked even softer and sweeter than usual.

"All of us do," Piper chimed in but Ethan was no longer looking at the whole group. He was right, his emotions showed all over the place. These ones didn't look sad at all.

Tia called it: "Dareen's. Strategy session. Tomorrow."

We straightened out the room and packed up our things quietly. Rae-Rae was humming something under her breath. "Ta da da dum da dum." Sunny flashed a momentary smile before we split up on the sidewalk. It wasn't until Ethan and Sunny turned down a side street and were out of earshot that Rae-Rae sang Fats Domino's words: "I want to walk you home." She explained, "Nobody sings sweet teenage love like The Fatman."

9

Being happy for Sunny and Ethan made me miss my techie. After I left the others, I took the bus over to his school. We live together—not like that—but it's still difficult to get time that's ours. Since he's placed with the Good Farmers too we don't think it's a good idea for anyone to learn about us. Mostly we try to meet up where no one knows both of us. Not that the Good Farmers would inform on us but the little kids that stay there sometimes, it's anyone's guess what they might say to whoever and we don't want to be split up. It makes us happy that we sleep under the same roof. Besides, not telling anyone anything is sort of a habit of mine.

Although we live at the same address our schools are miles apart. When you get placed, the Board of Ed has to ask if you want to stay in the same school. I hadn't. Hoke had. That was before he knew me.

As soon as my techie saw me he asked, "Why is my Anna limping?" I'd stiffened up on the bus ride over. I told him about my afternoon.

It had taken us a while to figure out good names for each other. One day he had asked me, "How's my girl?"

And I answered, "How's my boy?"

That made him laugh but it didn't solve the problem. He assured me, "I wouldn't mind if you called me 'my guy.' "

"And you call me 'my gal'?"

That made us *both* laugh. We experimented with "my boyfriend" and "my girlfriend" but that was too cringeworthy. "Sugar," "Honey," "Sweetie"—so not us. We settled finally on "my Anna" and "my Hoke." We like belonging to each other.

The first time Hoke had heard me talking about "my techie" he was a little offended, like how come he'd never heard of this new friend of mine? I still tease him about how dense that was. That's when he started threatening to call me his "un-techie."

It's not that I'm a complete dolt on a computer but it's not my language the way it's his.

"So, my Anna," Hoke asked, bringing me back to our conversation, "have you decided what you want to do?"

"I've decided that right now more than anything I want you to put your arms around me."

He grinned and led me off to as much privacy as we could find in his high school. Which wasn't much.

The first time Hoke had hugged me, he had just finished up months of "community service," clearing brush from roadsides. Whenever the county needs temp work done they hand out community service for just about any kind of trouble that kids like us get into. "Kids like us" means ones who don't have parents who might litigate. My lawyer taught me that word. It means fight back in court.

Anyway I doubt Hoke had done much physical labor before then. I don't think he had a clue how strong it made him. When he'd hugged me that first time, he held me so tight that it made me hug him back as hard as I could. It was the best feeling ever.

10

At our talk-it-out meeting, I half-expected Sunny to pass around heart-shaped candies. But she was cool.

On to business. Much more serious business than we'd originally signed on for. Rae-Rae made us laugh by singing an angry, defiant version of Elvis Presley's "Heartbreak Hotel." She made it sound like we could send Beemer there.

"But that's the question," Tia corrected. "We have to decide whether we want to try to make that happen."

"This time, why don't you go first?" I asked our parliamentarian. I could see Tia's eyes shift off-focus at the interruption and then sharp-focus as she concentrated on her answer.

"You all know me. I like order. It has . . . symmetry. I know I'm different, but in an ordered world there is a rightful place for me. I think when anyone misuses power, the piece of the world they occupy is thrown off balance and then my place gets crowded out. We all like Ethan but it is for personal reasons that I vote Beemer as our first OBaaT."

"Tia, if I understand what you just said, I admire it deeply," our warrior Dareen responded, "but those are not my reasons."

"For?" Tia asked, comfortably back to being parliamentarian.

"For also voting for Beemer. I guess we've all done a lot of thinking about this overnight. We already know from what happened with I-Hate-Bullies that Beemer has clout. The first thing I thought of is my sister gloating if OBaaT gets me into trouble at home. But my sister isn't capable of truly respecting my mother and grandmother. Sure, they might be angry, but underneath they'll be proud too. They sacrifice for me to not face hardships. It's not because they want me to have things. They want me to have *freedoms*. Like the freedom to not be a silenced witness."

Dareen looked uncomfortable as if she'd said more than she'd intended. Sunny slid her past the moment by chiming in: "Same here! My parents will have a cow but they'll get over it." Then her face fell as she turned in my direction. "But Anna, what about you? What happens if worst comes to worst and we get kicked out of school?"

"I don't know," I admitted in a voice too uncertain for my self-image. "I guess I might wind up in a new placement. That wouldn't be that terrible"—*I hope*—"except missing the people I care about if they move me too far away."

"Pledge!" Tia interrupted the sympathy coming my way. "I pledge to you Anna that no matter what happens, you will always be my friend and you will always be family."

Sunny jumped in eagerly: "I pledge to you Anna that no matter *what* happens, you will *always* be my friend and you will *always* be family."

Rae-Rae grinned, bouncing on her toes while she promised, "I pledge to you Anna that no matter whatever, you will always be my friend and you will always be family."

Dareen bowed. "I pledge to you Anna that no matter what"—a look of protective anger crossed her face—"you will always be my friend and you will always be family."

Piper held my hand and looked me straight in the eyes, standing proud like the old pre-Lance Piper I'd missed lately. "I pledge to you Anna that no matter what happens, you will always be my friend and you will always be family."

Closed-off Jade shocked me by crying while she vowed, "I pledge to you Anna that no matter what happens, I will always be your friend and you will always be my family."

My turn, to finish it. It was hard to get the words out. "I pledge to all of you that no matter what happens, you will always be my friends and you will always be my family."

Sunny slipped a box of heart-shaped sugar cookies out of her backpack and passed them around. "I wanted to get those Sweethearts candies"—*I knew it!*—"but I couldn't find them." We let her get away with that explanation without asking questions, but she blushed anyway.

"Back to voting," Tia announced after our break.

"I vote Beemer," Rae-Rae said. "Then I get to say 'Let's Rock.'"

Piper laughed and added, "I vote Beemer because he's a symbol to the rest of the bullies."

"Ethan's my friend," Jade said quietly. "I vote Beemer."

Sunny could have said "ditto" but she didn't. "I thought a lot about this because I wanted to be sure I was deciding for the right reasons. I joined OBaaT because I hate bullies hurting my friends. It's about the bullies not the friends, right? I vote Beemer because he's the biggest bully we know."

I was so proud of all of them I almost made it unanimous but I wasn't ready to. "Here's what I think," I answered when Tia called on me. "I'd like to go after Beemer but Tia is right. He is powerful. He will be worse if we try and fail. I think we should only go after him if we have enough to take him down. Right now we don't. We can complain that he says mean things and upsets kids—but who's going to take that seriously? What makes sense to me is we see what we can find out."

"Like ask around?" Tia wanted to know.

"Once when I had to go to court"—*Please don't ask why*—"my lawyer had me keep a notebook of things that had happened. Not like a journal but specific entries. As much as I could, she wanted each entry to have a date and even a time if possible, everybody who was there, a place, what was said, what was done, like that. That's what I think we should do about Beemer. We can try going backward as best we can. Going forward, every time we learn of anything that might be a useful entry we search out everything we can and write it down. Then we reconvene," I nodded to Tia, "and decide where to take it from there."

Tia pulled out a gavel I didn't know she had and said, "Done!"

And then her poem:

> Sometimes
> Justice
> is just
> Just us

11

We were all nervous about how to act when Beemer would start picking on someone but he didn't. All week long he was surprisingly . . . well, not him. Ethan started off our notebook with some past incidents. And OBaaT agreed, after only minimally teasing me, to have my techie see if he could find anything about Beemer online. Then we were all busy with midterm tests and papers before gratefully sinking into three whole days off for State-mandated school building sanitation before classes resumed.

Every one of those days off we practiced at the studio. Ethan worked us as hard as we could manage. It got so we knew the order of our reaction times. Dareen first, then Tia a fraction of a second later, then me, then everyone at once. We stopped being as sore after each practice.

Ethan was good at explaining. Like why we needed to practice so much. "Anna, when you walk shelter dogs, are any of them pit bulls?"

I didn't want it to show how uncomfortable I was that he'd spilled to my friends that I volunteer at the shelter. So I made a point of sounding cheerful: "Are you kidding? Most of them are!"

"You ever wrestle with any of them?"

"They love that! But they always win and they wear me out so sometimes I let them wrestle each other. I'm not supposed to, but I keep a close eye on them. Pits are easy because the hair stands up on their necks when they feel aggressive which lets me know when to step in and separate them quickly. Most always though they're only having fun."

I stopped myself, surprised I'd talked that much.

Ethan saved me by getting back on topic: "Yes, pit bulls have an innate sense of kinetics. There are two of them who play in a yard on my block and I watch them whenever I can. They actually seem to study each other's moves and think up counters."

Sunny asked for us: "Ethan what does that mean, 'an innate sense of kinetics'?"

He nodded to himself and explained, "They understand instinctively how bodies move. It's no longer genetically encoded in our species. We humans will never have that skill again which is why all martial arts developed from the study of animals. Instead of instinct, we have to practice to have . . . muscle memory that comes as close as we can."

Afterward Jade asked me quietly if she could come with me to the shelter sometime to walk the dogs. She looked . . . not quite as defensive as usual.

"Yes."

Piper found a news story about a ten-year-old who was being bullied online. We used OBaaT's Facebook page to write her mother, offering to post positive, supportive messages. The mother could check what we wrote before letting her daughter see it. It took several days to get any answer at all and then it was an "invitation" from the mother to contribute to the daughter's GoFundMe page. NoThankYou.

I whispered a question to Dareen about her sister. "Great news!" she announced to all of us. "She completed all the requirements for early graduation. She worked it so she gets to start a semester early in her precious Feminist Studies Department—that combined BA/MA/PhD program. Like feminism is about books, not battles."

"Couldn't it be both?" Tia asked after a pause.

"Not for the know-it-all." Dareen sighed, admitted: "My mother agrees with you. She says there are different legitimate paths. My grandmother agrees with me, but she respects my mother's decision not to intervene between us." Dareen shook off being diverted: "Anyway, my sister moves out January 2. I won't ever, ever, ever again have to live with her telling me every day how much better and smarter and more enlightened than me she is." *One less OBaaT.*

Dareen being more open than usual inspired Sunny to ask her if she wanted to do a sleepover.

"Why?"

"I'm sorry," Sunny apologized. "I thought that would be the easiest way to get you out of your apartment at night."

"No. You don't understand." Dareen debated with herself, thought it through, tried to explain to us: "It's true I live with . . . restrictions that the rest of you don't. But out of respect, not disrespect. My mother and my grandmother have taught me to assess situations for danger and take only what risks I feel are important."

Tia bowed like her teacher had. From the waist, arms at her sides, honoring Dareen.

Dareen seemed more with us after what she'd said. Even with what OBaaT tried next.

Actually, it was Jade who had to make up something to get permission to go with us. She didn't share what that was.

When I heard our destination I must have looked suspiciously at my cargo pants and hoodie. All of us were wearing our personal uniforms. Piper grinned and quickly invited us home with her.

When we got to the condo, a note chalked onto a blackboard door in the kitchen said Piper's mother was out somewhere I didn't think was my business to read. Even with her mom gone, I felt like I shouldn't touch anything—it was that kind of place. Piper's dad's was way more relaxed but Piper's Closet—really it was more like a huge mirrored dressing room—was at her mother's.

Piper waved her arm in invitation and we all dove into treasure-hunting for each other. Finding sizes for all of us was no problem because Piper's mom insisted on holding on to the "good clothes" even after Piper outgrew them. Plus lately Piper had started wearing lots of oversized layers. So much so that it was starting to feel like more than a fashion choice.

Sunny looked longingly at a flouncy pastel pink dress that was a fancied-up version of what she'd normally wear—but Jade handed her a red velvet tank and slinky lattice-hem leggings instead. They bargained back and forth until Jade let Sunny substitute some deep blue Palazzo pants for the leggings.

Sunny tried to pay Jade back by picking the flouncy dress for her, but Jade looked so miserable in pink that Piper handed her black trousers and a matching black turtleneck instead. I couldn't remember the last time I'd seen Jade in anything more colorful.

Tia usually went for a man-tailored flannel shirt over yoga pants. I found her a denim overall skirt with a cute mahogany T-shirt underneath and she smiled her thanks that I hadn't gone too girlie. Piper gave me an approving raised eyebrow that the tee blended in so beautifully with Tia's maple syrup–colored skin.

Dareen never showed any skin. I think that was part of her culture. Sunny found her a long-sleeved silk jumpsuit in a deep coral that brought some rosiness to Dareen's olive complexion.

Rae-Rae was the easiest to dress because she loved every new look no matter what. She didn't really have go-to clothes like the rest of us although she'd invented a look of long-sleeved crop top over paint-spattered skinny jeans that she loved to vogue. Tia indulged Rae-Rae's preference for variety with a stretchy animal print short-sleeve crop top over a vertical-striped mini skirt that she'd unearthed from Piper's "too small" collection.

We were all intimidated trying to dress the only one of us who actually knew fashion but Piper always oohed appreciatively whatever we chose. Without really consulting each other we layered her in a bunch of different purples in silky fabrics which Rae-Rae topped with a floppy oversized hat that I'd never seen Piper wear before. If she understood that we knew she wanted oversized but weren't asking why, Piper didn't let it show.

That left me. I was always a group project. I knew they meant well, figuring that it was a treat for me to get out of my budget-limited wardrobe. If I let myself relax enough, it was. Piper picked out a simple lemon-yellow sundress. Sunny found a shaggy little pale blue shrug to put over it. Tia tied a gold scarf as a belt at my waist. Jade found me a pretty jade-green ring. Dareen chose some stretchy pink ballet slippers for my feet. Rae-Rae brought it all together with a huge flower-stenciled hobo bag. It was hard not to feel like Cinderella.

With all of us prettied-by-Piper, Rae-Rae paraded us into teen-night at a local club to see the band she'd told us about. As soon as they were on break we swarmed all over the musicians, making a point of ignoring the lead singer. Rae-Rae was right, of course. The guy was a jerk. But we were not convinced the rest of the band were a whole lot better. The epic part of the night was when Rae-Rae talked the manager into letting us onstage between sets. Rae-Rae handed us each a kazoo, shouted "Thank you Dion!" and we performed a blues kazoo instrumental of "Little Diane." The manager had a sense of humor so after the audience cheered our instrumental, he played Cyndi Lauper on the sound system and let us all dance around to "Girls Just Want to Have Fun." '80s, but just right for that night.

13

By the time school resumed Beemer was back to normal. Normal for him, I mean. Nothing in any of our classes, but by the end of the week we had pages in our notebook about him again picking on a kid who stutters, a fat kid with really bad b.o., and a Spanish kid who hadn't done his homework. None of it surprised us, which was the most disturbing part. It made us realize how much we'd fallen into accepting Beemer's bullying as "it is what it is."

Jade met me after class Thursday to go to the shelter. I hadn't been sure if she would and I wasn't sure I would like it. The first thing she asked me was whether I'd ever had a dog.

"No."

"Me either . . . How did you learn how to walk them?"

"Oh Jade, don't worry. It's easy and I'll show you how."

Once we were both reassured the conversation was going to be limited to the topic of dogs, she had a million questions and I surprised myself by having a lot of answers.

"Why do you take a bus to the shelter on Greene Street, Anna? Isn't there a closer one?"

"Greene Street is a no-kill shelter." Jade looked upset by the phrase. "Yeah, I know. It's hard to think about. There are so many healthy, lovely animals whose lives are taken from them by what they call 'shelters.' Some places, I don't think I could ever volunteer at. The place we're going to, it took me a while to find them but they're good people. They're kind. Even if they have a dog that can never be adopted out—like fear biters who can't be trusted around people—they keep them and give them good lives. The dogs you'll meet though, it's Greene Street's goal to find them all homes."

"Will they interview me? Like do I have to pass a test or something?"

"They know me. I'm guessing it'll be as simple as you coming along but we'll ask, OK?"

"What kind of dog do you think they'll give me?"

"I'll suggest one of the seniors for you to start with. Like Lilly-Belle, she's a total sweetie-pie and so old she just pokes along."

"I hope she likes me."

"Oh Jade, wait'll you see!"

Once we got to our destination bus stop, Jade reverted to quiet. We turned off the street into a fenced-in setback that surrounded a shabby old house. One of the reasons I had picked the Greene Street shelter is how clean it smells when you walk in. Real clean, like just-washed. Not that bleachy-over-bad smell. There's nothing shabby about the people who work there either. Or the dogs.

It turned out Jade did have to fill out some paperwork and get approved. I guess that's right. They shouldn't let just anybody walk off with a dog. One of the attendants disappeared into the back and returned with Lilly-Belle already on a leash.

Before we went anywhere all three of us sat on the floor while Lilly-Belle and Jade had a proper introduction. Even squatted down, Jade looked sharp-edged. Slowly, some small piece of the tension within her gave way to accommodate Lilly-Belle's soft circles. The dog is a funny-looking barrel-bodied little brown thing. She has stubby legs and puddly paws that make me laugh and solemn, round, cloudy eyes that have the opposite effect. Jade's face when Lilly-Belle licked it tilted the balance toward laughter.

Although it took no kind of expertise to walk Lilly-Belle, I showed Jade how to hold a leash properly and how to match the dog's pace. With Lilly-Belle that was a kind of slo-mo lesson. Still, the old mutt had a grand time on our walk and returned to the shelter with her tail wagging waltztime. Jade's shadows had receded a little as well.

"Will you come with me while I take out one of the bigger dogs?" I asked Jade.

"Sure," she answered without realizing what she was letting herself in for.

The attendant got Rocky for me. This time we did the introductions standing up. Rocky is a Rottweiler-and-who-knows-what mix who way outweighs me and Jade together. Jade's eyes got big when she saw him charging toward us but she seemed to get that he meant no harm. The thing is, Rocky loves every living creature. Affection and excitement kind of burst out of his whole, huge furry being. If you can hold on to him, he's great fun to walk.

Rocky's exercise took much longer than Lilly-Belle's and we covered a lot more distance. By the time we were done, we were done in. On the bus back, Jade reverted to being her masked-over self, but still she asked me to tell her next time I went to the shelter.

Well, that worked.

14

The next meeting at Dareen's we filled a whole new page in the Beemer notebook before Rae-Rae trudged in. No bounce. No song. Tia continued the note-taking about Beemer, giving Rae-Rae a chance to tell us, but nothing . . . until it was evident we were done for the day, and then Rae-Rae was matter-of-fact.

"Anna, you need to pick up your safe phone from the police precinct. This is the address."

She handed me a crumpled scrap of paper. I looked her a question.

"The new girl. Charity. She ran away."

"Has she told you where she is?" Tia asked.

"No." Rae-Rae's voice cracked. "She didn't even tell me she was running. She left behind the phone Anna gave her. The cops checked it to see who she had contacted. I was the only one."

Rae-Rae's words seeped around the ache in her voice: "The cops wanted to know if I was hiding her, knew where she was, or had heard from her at all since she ran. All the cop questions. The only reason they dropped it was 'cause they could tell—

46

before I stopped letting on anything—how surprised I'd been by the news."

"Rae-Rae, none of this is your fault," Sunny tried to comfort her.

"My sister always tells me 'You can't save everyone,' " Rae-Rae said bitterly. "But I know what she really means. That I'm about to *inconvenience* her by trying."

"Yeah," Dareen acknowledged, "your sister's cold."

"It's not that," Rae-Rae corrected Sunny's reassurance. "Truly, I don't feel bad for me, like I should have acted differently. It's only . . . it makes me sad that Charity is so . . . *alone.*"

"We all feel like that," I answered, meaning it about more than the new girl. "But all we can do is offer. People have to want to, be ready to be . . . not alone."

I had planned to visit my Hoke after our meeting. Instead I found myself telling Jade I was headed for the shelter, did she want to come?

When they brought Lilly-Belle out, the little mutt ran right over to Jade and licked her. Jade squealed, "She remembered me!" I love dogs.

. . .

OBaaT assembled in the back room of the studio, waiting. Of all people, it was Tia who was late. She marched in stone-faced. Ethan was right behind her, tears leaking out of his eyes. Neither one of them had changed into workout clothes.

"Beemer's done it," Tia announced. "He went too far." *Nothing in her voice sounds like a victory.*

Ethan took up the story: "You know that kid they call 'Willy' although his real name isn't William?"

We all looked blank.

Tia clarified, "Frail? Not really there?"

That could be a lot of people. Ethan shrugged and returned to telling us what had happened. "I hate to call him 'Willy' but I don't know his real name. Anyway, he tries to disappear in Beemer's class. I guess a lot of us do. But Willy is always in Beemer's line of sight."

Ethan paused, shuddered, continued: "Today during third period Beemer made Willy stand at the front of the class while Beemer projected Willy's midterm on that overhead screen he loves to use. The exam paper was all marked up in red. Beemer went through it, answer by answer, sentence by sentence saying how stupid it was, mocking, venomous."

We gasped, imagining how any of us would feel if that had happened to us.

"Willy was so humiliated," Ethan whispered. "It was . . . abhorrent." He spit the word out. "I tried to change the subject but Beemer shut me up and went back to torturing Willy. Then I tried to object—I said, 'Mr. Beemer, you're really upsetting him'—that's when Beemer threw me out of class. I told the principal—I mean The Tsar—what was going on but he only wanted to lecture me on mouthing off in class."

Tia took up the story: "I wasn't there but I guess Beemer continued, getting meaner and meaner to Willy for the whole class. The way I heard it, Willy just stood there, trembling. He never said anything or tried to defend himself."

"Yes, that's right." Ethan nodded solemnly, like that was the first time the degree of Willy's defenselessness had fully registered to him.

Tia filled in her own piece: "I had to go to the administrative offices after fifth period. Before I could ask the secretary anything, Beemer's student-teacher intern came running in breathless, sent the nurse to that bathroom near the storage lockers that no one goes to. Then the teacher intern called 911 to dispatch them there too. 'Student, male, 15, about 5'4", 120 pounds, found unconscious for possibly several hours, cause undetermined.' Then the intern turned to the room in general to explain how she'd figured out that no one had seen Willy since Beemer's class and went looking for him. The student-teacher intern looked expectant but no one responded. They sort of stumbled around, stunned silent. Not one of them noticed me until after the ambulance came and took Willy away. Then they told me I didn't belong there and rushed me out quick. When I left, The Tsar was closeted up with Beemer. Neither one of them looked happy."

Tia paused, letting Ethan explain that he'd met up with her outside the administrative offices. All the kids still in the building had wanted to know what was going on with the ambulance. Ethan and Tia had compared notes and come straight here. While Ethan was talking, Tia began to cry. Still, she called the session to order and tried to get practice going.

Our hearts weren't in it. No matter how much we pounded the mats, it felt pointless.

We were too late. We'd failed. Before we'd even started.

15

The official word—passed through unofficial channels—the next day was that Willy had had a seizure. He was still in the hospital but he would recover. Mr. Beemer and his student-teacher intern were both absent. A sub taught his classes. Small comfort.

Still, as the days passed with no sign of Beemer, OBaaT started to feel like maybe they'd fire him. Maybe his reign of pain was finally over.

I think it was because we'd half-convinced ourselves that was true, that's why it hit us so hard when a week later Beemer was back in class as if nothing had happened.

I knew I was letting my friends down even more but I felt like The Tsar and all of them had frozen me inside myself. I stopped trying. I didn't want to see anyone or do anything. Each morning I walked out of the Good Farmers' as if I was going to school. Then I circled back to the shed and hid in there until it was time to "return" from school. Mostly I slept because that was the easiest way not to think or feel.

I might have gone on like that for a long time except that the holidays came up fast. The little kids were, as usual, short-termers and already placed elsewhere. The second the winter school break started, the Good Farmers dropped the rest of us off. I barely had time to pack my I-can't-lose-this possessions.

At least it's a no-kill shelter, I thought to myself sadly. I can do self-pity really well when I try.

16

Still, it was hard to maintain that level of wallowing in a building that had witnessed so much misery. Even with only a few residents during the holidays, the despair smell off the dinge-colored walls reminded me how many kids had it worse than me.

By the third day, I was more relieved than I wanted to admit to myself when Ethan's older brother Gabe showed up to sign me out for the day. If you didn't know him, Gabe could pass as a "responsible adult."

It thawed my sadness to see Ethan waiting for me on the sidewalk. "Glad to see you," he told me.

Sunny popped up from behind him. "Glad to see her?" she teased Ethan. "A genius-level vocabulary and that's the best you can come up with?

"We couldn't stand missing you one more minute!" she announced as she handed me a humongous Snickers wrapped with a big purple bow. "This is for you!

"And if you like that, we have an even better surprise waiting for you in Gabe's car!" *Please don't be a giant chocolate Santa.*

Sunny flung open the door and gestured to its contents with a flourish. "Your techie!"

I was so happy to see him it took me a moment to react. "How did you know?"

"Oh, Anna," Sunny sighed at me. "We've always known. We just didn't know his name."

(My Hoke explained to me later that when I had dropped out of sight their paths had crossed looking for me.)

"I'm sorry," I said to all of them, "for everything—"

"—Nope," Sunny cut me off, "not happening. Today is a celebration. Everybody voted and I get to decide the whole day."

I surprised myself by giggling. "Oh I'm sure that was so democratic," I teased, slipping more easily than I could have imagined into her mood. "Ethan here is smitten. What wouldn't he say 'yes' to you about? And Hoke, you've probably terrorized him already."

"I'm not afraid," Hoke promised Sunny. *No, I've never seen you afraid of anything. Well, except maybe about losing me.*

Gabe made one of those "get on with it" noises so Sunny gave him directions.

"We're going to that museum," she explained to him pointing on the map on her phone and ignoring our groans. "You can pick us all up there at 4:00 this afternoon."

"Yes, ma'am," he muttered, not grumpy enough to sound like he actually objected. He gave his brother a you-owe-me look when he dropped us off.

. . .

The sidewalk was wide enough for all four of us to walk alongside each other, bumping hips and shoulders like puppies. It felt . . . festive.

We walked inside a building-sized marble entrance with the highest ceilings I've ever seen. A sign caught my eye about the admission fee. I felt for my wallet and student ID, worried about having enough money. Sunny knocked me softly on my temple with her knuckles, reading my mind and silently telling me not to worry.

She steered us around the line queuing for admittance, heading toward a set of double doors. A small sign read "Museum Restaurant." Inside it was filled with sunlight from floor-to-ceiling windows that looked out on a kind of winter garden. It smelled like bacon and pastries. There were dozens of what Piper had once told me were called "café table sets" with round, open metalwork. The greeter who told us to "sit anywhere" and the ones who waited on us all wore badges that said "Museum Volunteer."

Sunny proudly promised that we were going to have "the best breakfast ever."

Before opening the menu I'd figured I'd order toast, already having eyeballed the jam on the table. But when I looked at the prices, I couldn't believe how cheap everything was. At the bottom of the menu it said, "All menu items hand-prepared by museum volunteers. All proceeds and tips go to defray the costs of the ongoing operations of the museum."

"Pancakes!" The word popped out of me the second a Volunteer-badged man came over to take our order. Hoke sounded overjoyed ordering sausage and eggs and home fries. Sunny spotted a mastodon-sized berry muffin with crumb top-ping that she soon literally used wet fingers to vacuum off her plate. Ethan, being Ethan, ordered something healthy-looking that the rest of us refused to look at.

Ethan admired all our plates of food and pronounced deadpan, "This is definitely not a Snarf-N-Go."

"Ethan," I shouted, "who knew you were funny!" I didn't mean to embarrass him. I was laughing too hard to think.

"I've always had a sense of humor but I never admitted it before—"

"—Sunny," I finished for him. "You guys are so good together."

"Us too," Hoke spoke under his breath. I hadn't thought breakfast could get any better.

"OK, you were right," I acknowledged to Sunny when I'd polished clean everything down to the last smear of syrup. "On to the exhibits?"

To all our relief, Sunny shook her head. Sometimes I like looking at beautiful things but it didn't feel that kind of day. "You all underestimate me," Sunny boasted.

"Do you mind then," I asked her, "I'm stuffed—could we take a walk?"

"You forget I've eaten here before." Sunny beamed at me. "Next on our agenda if you want to, I thought we'd walk shelter dogs?"

"Sunny, you're afraid of dogs!" I objected.

But she just smiled. "Ethan will protect me."

Ethan squared his shoulders and tried to look like "of course" but he couldn't quite pull it off. Still, they insisted and I wanted to so much I said, "Yes."

. . .

When we got there Greene Street's front offices were quiet, one of those rare lulls that lets everyone catch up. The shelter manager was on duty, I guessed because she'd taken someone's shift to free them for the holidays. I introduced my friends. Looking at them, she apologized that Rocky was on one of his many tryout days.

People always fall in love with Rocky before they learn how difficult his exuberance can be to contain. He's been sent on so many trials with potential adopters I think he's come to view them as simply day adventures. At least I hope so.

"Don't worry," the Greene Street shelter manager assured my worried-looking companions, "Voss doesn't want to see anyone today." *Everyone assumes I tell my friends more than I do.*

When the shelter manager noticed their confusion she explained: "Voss is a magnificent animal. A white Akita so beautiful and fearsome . . ." She caught herself getting lost in regret for the dog. "Some subhuman must have done very ugly things to him. He lives to exact revenge. He can never be trusted around any man and there are only a few women he responds to. We were shocked when it turned out he liked Anna talking to him and admiring him, but we shouldn't have been." She smiled gently at me.

"What will happen to him?" Ethan asked her, fearful of her answer.

"We'll make sure he has a good life," she answered defensively. Then, as if she realized Ethan hadn't meant to doubt Greene Street, she explained: "We meet every dog's needs as best we can. Voss can never be adopted but he can have what suits him. Most of the time all he wants is to be left in peace. He has a dog-defensible living space, self-watering and feeding set-ups, his own dog run. Self-sufficiency is what makes him happy."

"That's a lot better than what Ruben wants!" I told her, loyal to Voss.

"Ruben is just plain rotten," the shelter manager laughed, explaining to the others: "He hates children. It's . . . pathological. He's a big-muscled Dobie so ordinarily they'd stay away from him but he . . . It's like, he deliberately lures them in looking sad and appealing. His sole goal is to get them within range. Somebody must have allowed children to torment him. We haven't totally given up on the idea he might be trained out of it, but he's too stubborn. Most likely he'll be another lifer here."

"But if he's dangerous ..."

"Look, Sunny is it? Cute, cuddly pups are not the only dogs who need to be rescued. In some ways, they need us less. True rescue is about recognizing that living beings have value and giving them the best life that we can given who they are. Most often if that's difficult to do it is because some horrific human has made them that way."

Beside me, Hoke nodded.

The shelter manager offered me Thug to walk. After the conversation we'd just had, Sunny kind of paled at the name. It was perfect timing that Jade arrived for what I found out was her daily (*!*) Lilly-Belle walk. Some visible magic was happening between them. The only time Jade ever seemed like the person I knew, Lilly-Belle was with her. Ethan and Sunny ambled off gratefully with our friend and her friend, promising to meet up when Hoke and I were done with Thug.

Hoke laughed out loud when they brought Thug into the waiting area. "A cocker spaniel! Really?!"

"Shhh!" I whispered. "Nobody's told him he's a cocker spaniel."

Hoke looked more closely. Thug gave him the hairy eyeball, hunched down on his muscular legs with a "What?!" challenge in his poised, stunted body. Hoke snorted while I hooked Thug up. The leash has an extra ring so I can wrap it around the dog's waist for added control.

"C'mon, Thug," I cajoled, scratching behind his ears. He tolerated me . . . as long as no other dogs were around to witness the moment of weakness.

"Maybe 'Thug' isn't the best name for a dog they're hoping to get adopted," the ever-logical Hoke offered.

"Truth in advertising," the shelter manager answered for me, winking.

Thug thoroughly enjoyed his trot-walk punctuated by barking at every dog within sniffing distance. He is an athletic little guy. It took us some serious walking to wear him out. By the time we got back, Jade was long gone and Ethan and Sunny were sitting on a bench down the street from the shelter. They didn't look like they'd minded having time for just the two of them.

. . .

"Do you need to do any shopping?" Sunny asked, shooting a "don't even" look at Ethan and Hoke.

"Buddhist, remember?"

I appreciated Sunny offering me the opportunity to buy holiday gifts. She grinned to let me know she understood my answer that I still didn't do Christmas. But Ethan and Hoke looked totally confused and, since they hadn't asked, I filled them in.

"When I was little one of my first memories was hating Christmastime. There'd be all these ... dignitaries, bearing sacks of generic wrapped presents, smiling self-satisfied as long as the cameras were rolling. Even that young we knew our job was to look all grateful and excited."

I glanced at Hoke. He knew.

"Anyway, I always tried to get out of it as politely as I could. One year some church lady asked me incredulously, 'Don't you like Christmas? It's Our Lord's birthday. What kind of a Christian are you?' If I hadn't been angry I probably would have stayed quiet."

Sunny is such a great audience that she started giggling, knowing that what was coming took the sting off.

"I blurted out—I still don't know where this came from— 'I'm a Buddhist.' I didn't even know what a Buddhist was! I must have heard the word sometime and liked the sound of it. I don't think the church lady believed me but a social worker from the state overheard and took it *really* seriously. She yelled at the church lady!

"After that, they didn't make me participate in Christmas. But word must have come down to accommodate my 'faith' and all that fussing created its own problems. Once they even tried to bus me over to a temple to celebrate a Buddhist holiday. 'Accommodating' must have been a whole lot of extra work for the state because they quickly accepted it when I protested 'I'm not *that* kind of Buddhist.' "

Sunny held up her hand to stop me because Ethan was choking from trying not to laugh. Even my Hoke was kind of spluttering. It felt so good being with my friends.

After that, Sunny took us over to the used bookstore on Seventh. We each went to different sections, spending the next couple of hours browsing and reading and checking in with each other. Then Sunny asked us if it was OK to stop by her house, where she ran in and then came back out hauling a huge picnic basket she'd had all ready for us. Ethan and Hoke lugged it over to the park and although it was getting kind of cold by then, and I couldn't believe I could be hungry after the breakfast we'd had, it was a true picnic.

. . .

"What now, Sunny?" Ethan asked half teasing/half expectant. She was ready for him.

"The squirrel lady!" Sunny announced triumphantly.

"You *can't* mean that crazy lady who dresses up squirrels and holds shows with them?!" Hoke's orderly brain couldn't quite take in the concept.

"That's exactly what I mean," Sunny assured him. "You'll see."

It was a long walk but we needed to warm up anyway. Ethan and Hoke tried unsuccessfully to practice not-laughing faces while we trooped over to an odd little crooked street. We spotted a house tucked back behind a big twisted tree. Each wall of the house was painted a different primary color with contrasting bits of brightness for the roof and the part above the front door. There was lots of foot traffic and cars parked around it. Turns out, we arrived in the middle of a show.

A box by the door invited us to leave the entry fee, with graduating prices based on age. The top price was only $4.00 but my techie did a quick calculation in his head, something about average audience size and age and number of shows per week. After he got through explaining the variables all I got out of it was that the squirrel lady seemed to be doing pretty well for herself, "for a crazy person," he added under his breath.

When we caught up to her, the squirrel lady was decked out extremely colorfully herself with painted-on makeup in bold shades on her ageless face. As she explained each tableau her voice had a kind of lilt to it although she was trying to sound serious. Something about how she interacted with the crowd was like "I know you're laughing at me but that's really all right."

We'd joined halfway through. I don't know what had come before but our host was in the middle of displaying Sir Squirrel Lancelot, complete with belted tunic and boots. No sword though. I guess it's not a good idea to give squirrels edged weapons. Like all the other squirrels, once the crowd's attention was focused on him, he sat alertly on his haunches. On command, Sir Squirrel Lancelot bowed low to Lady Squirrel Guinevere, who was quite ornamental in a long flowy purple gown. Her little squirrel ears twitched as she acknowledged her suitor's greeting.

Then there was Wonder Squirrel Woman in red, white and blue. I guess to give equal time to the feminist squirrels.

There were so many displays that I don't remember them all but one of my favorites was a whole family of Squirrel Incredibles with skin-tight red and black stretchy body suits and black masks. They were an assortment of sizes and even posed off—sort of— in The Incredibles' fight gestures, hard to do since they were still squatted down for balance. Of course, they were accompanied by Edna Mode Squirrel who had a black wig, big black glasses, and a high-couture ensemble. Something about her reminded me of the squirrel lady herself.

We were the only teenagers in a crowd filled mostly with little kids and their parents. They oohed and aahed at all the right times but toward the end, you could tell they were getting tired. Finally the tour concluded and they all tromped out. The squirrel lady turned to Sunny with a "give me a minute" request. She came back in five, having changed into jeans and a sweatshirt, with the gloop washed off her face. She asked for Sunny's help undressing all the squirrels.

As soon as they were liberated from their costumes, the rodents stretched their little bodies out into their freedom. Released into a large back room they ran around what looked like squirrel play-heaven. Sunny slid a window partway open in the back for them to venture into an outdoor area if they preferred. Done with the tasks, our host invited us all into the kitchen for tea. I don't drink tea but it seemed like the right thing for the occasion.

We had plenty of questions but she looked tired so we tried not to swamp her. The way she sank and luxuriated into her chair reminded me of the squirrels greeting their playroom. Sunny introduced her as Mrs. Birdfoot although I don't know if that was a stage name or her real name. She told us to call her Mamie.

At Mamie's request, Sunny passed around mugs of cinnamon-y sweet tea and homemade molasses cookies while we cozied up to an actual kitchen table. When Mamie was as comfortable as she'd made all of us, she told us her story. None of us interrupted, not wanting her to stop.

"When I retired, I didn't know what to do with myself," Mamie began. She sighed, remembering. "I think I spent days looking out this kitchen window. Eventually I realized there was a lot going on out there if you took the time to see it. And time was what I had plenty of. My health, thank god, was still good. I own this house free and clear and my needs are small enough for my pension to keep me going. But I didn't know for what.

"One day, I'm not sure why, I decided to put up a birdfeeder. What do I know about feeding birds? I threw in a bunch of different seeds and nuts and hoped for the best. Some little birds—chickadees I think—ate up all the smallest seeds but the remainder were too big a challenge for them. For a few days there was a family of chipmunks. Oh my goodness they were too cute! But they moved on. There was a raccoon for a time but the neighbors were up in arms and made him feel unwelcome. Then the squirrels came. More and more of them. I kept filling the feeder but it never seemed like enough! After a while, I was buying peanuts by the 26-pound bag."

Mamie paused to take a sip of her tea, smiling at her own foolishness.

"The squirrels were lively and entertaining but I still felt out of place in this world. Then one day, a baby squirrel fell out of a tree and injured its leg. I ran into the yard, wrapped him in a towel, and brought him inside with me. I looked up everything I could find about how to help him. The predictions were all somewhat dire but I think my baby squirrel must not have been as badly hurt as the ones they were talking about. He let me wrap up his little leg—I cut a tiny oblong from an ace bandage!—and let me feed him milk from an eyedropper. Looking back, I know I had no clue what I was doing but amazingly, the little guy survived."

Ethan had looked so worried during this part of the story that I felt a surge of relief at the outcome.

"I don't know whether that squirrel sent out the news among his species, or the squirrels around here are exceptionally injury- and illness-prone, or it was all pure coincidence. But after a while I had a regular Sciuridae Ward going. That's the official name for the species, by the way. Eventually word spread among humans too and people started bringing me any injured squirrel they found . . . it seemed like in the whole tri-state area."

Mamie checked our faces to see if she was losing her audience but we were totally listening.

"Let me tell you, they may be small but squirrels are not cheap. Especially when they need vet care. And to keep them on squirrel food! I mean I was glad to be taking care of little creatures that without me—I think most of them probably would not have made it—but I started worrying about how long I could afford to keep this up. I buckled down and did my homework to set up an official charity but—do you have *any* idea how hard it is to raise money for a squirrel rescue?"

Keep a straight face!

"I did interviews to try to publicize the charity. The squirrels were so very appealing that reporters would come to take pictures or video them. But interest burned out as soon as the novelty wore off.

"That's when I came up with the idea. When I was a child I loved sewing doll clothes and making dollhouse furniture. I made up some little squirrel hospital beds, with teeny, tiny, little white sheet sets." Mamie laughed then, one of those full-throated proud-of-yourself chortles that makes everyone happy. "And I put them in little flannel PJs. Once you get used to how pot-bellied their small bodies are, the clothes are easy to make. Anyhoo, making people laugh sure brought interest back around!"

Mamie snacked at her cookie and I tried not to think about how squirrel-like her nibbling looked.

"A lot of the interviewers, they clearly thought I was batty. I figured out that as long as I was good-humored about it, the nuttier I acted, the more popular the interview was. That's when I started with these performances. I don't show the sick squirrels anymore because I don't want to disturb them. Some of my recuperated patients, their injuries are permanent and they can't go back to the wild. As long as I can keep their little brains engaged, they don't seem to mind. And many of the healed ones like to stick around or come back to visit. I make sure they earn their peanuts while they're here. All of them, they're like a natural, ham-it-up acting troupe."

Mamie seemed mostly wound down by then so I asked, "Do you do all the training yourself?"

"Oh yes," she told us proudly. "I am the original and only Sciuridae performance coach."

I don't think I've ever met anybody better at not taking themselves seriously. A skill I definitely need to learn.

Ethan asked, "Sunny, how did you *find* her?" nodding his head toward Mamie.

"I saw Mamie interviewed on TV and I just had to come see for myself. Afterward, we got to chatting. Now, we're friends." Sunny smiled at Mamie shyly. Mamie grinned broadly in return.

We got back to the museum right as Ethan's brother Gabe was pulling up. Two of us were due back at our teen shelters. Hoke kept hold of my hand until almost the last minute. Sunny didn't want to hear it when I tried to thank her for the best day ever. Ethan was the last one to hug me when we got back to my teen shelter. He had tears in his eyes simply from having to say goodbye. I love that about him. About all of them.

17

When he brought me inside to sign me back in, Gabe helped me carry all the schoolwork Sunny had assembled for me to be able to catch up over the break. There was a probie—probationary shelter worker—at the front desk I hadn't seen before. Over the holidays they do skeleton crews with only one experienced person per shift on call as backup. It was hit-or-miss staffing and this probie was definitely in the "miss" category. I should have known better than to walk in smiling.

"Did we have fun?" she sneered at me before looking Gabe up and down appreciatively and—I swear this is true—licking her lips. Then she patted her butt and oozed to him, "Wouldn't you prefer someone with better *assets*?"

"That's all you got huh?" Gabe deadpanned.

I had to laugh. Maybe I'd underestimated Ethan's brother.

Miss Assets was not pleased. "I'll see you later," she warned me, conveying just how joyous my holiday season promised to be.

None of us had noticed that the shelter manager's door was open. I guess she'd been quietly catching up on paperwork on an off day. She poked her head out of it. "In here. Now!" she ordered the probie. The click of the door behind them sounded angry.

I left the tied-with-a-bow giant Snickers in the shelter manager's cubby with a post-it that said, "Thank you!"

Later that evening the shelter manager called me down to her office. Her name is Mrs. Meeny which always makes me think she is the most misnamed person ever. Handing me back the Snickers she explained, "I don't allow the staff to accept presents which means I don't either. But I kept the note." She smiled.

I like her. She's always straight with me.

"That's not the only reason I wanted to talk to you. You see what I have on staff right now." Mrs. Meeny grimaced. "Tomorrow we're getting a new admission, actually a readmission. You know the ropes, Anna. And you know how I want *all* our residents respected. It would really help me out if you would be willing to befriend her, make sure she's not mistreated. If anything isn't up to standard, please insist that the on-call person be notified."

I promised I would, proud to be asked.

18

When Mrs. Meeny had used the word "readmission" I had suspected, or maybe I had only hoped, but I wasn't totally surprised the next day when Rae-Rae's "new girl," Charity, was escorted into the shelter by two uniformed cops. They signed her in and then left so, good, she wasn't arrested or anything. There was a totally different probie on duty today. Overeager but at least not hostile. I volunteered to bring Charity up to the dorm rooms but the probie insisted on giving her a full tour. I tried to signal a hello to Charity but she was hustled off.

She looks better than I expected, I thought. *No bruises, not as skinny, and not as haunted. Not my business.*

There were so few of us over the holidays that we didn't really need to double up. I was surprised when the probie later introduced Charity to me as my "new roomie." When Charity requested her own room instead, I couldn't tell if she recognized me or not. Before she left though she turned to me at the door with a question: "Talk to you later?" I nodded.

Boring as it was, I needed to catch up on schoolwork. It had seemed like a lifetime but there were literally only four days of missed classes. Beemer had reappeared in all his slime on a Monday and the Good Farmers had deposited us at the various teen shelters Friday afternoon. I slogged my way through the missed assignments. It helped a lot that all my friends had taken notes and filled in the blanks of where each of our teachers wanted the material to take us. Except for a really confusing scrap of paper, the piles of homework didn't include any personal messages. It took me a while to figure out what Rae-Rae had meant when she wrote "Don't be Lesley Gore, be Brenda Lee." I looked up their hit song titles and eventually translated. Not the leave-me-alone of "It's my party and I'll cry if I want to," but instead letting them in because "I want to be wanted."

I had work to do.

. . .

The first thing Charity asked me was if I could reach out to Rae-Rae.

"Of course."

"I didn't want to get you guys in trouble. That's why I left your phone behind. But it killed me to give it up."

I hesitated about spilling it to Charity that I still had her safe phone. *Prove in.*

Charity stacked the books spread over my bed onto my dorm desk and lay down beside me. Normally I don't like strangers in my space but the way she did it, it felt like one of the shelter dogs burrowing in for comfort.

"Don't hate me," she asked softly.

"Look," I said, trying for gentle. "I don't *know* you." *Mistake. If she tells me her story, she'll want to know mine.* "I assume you had your reasons."

"I did," she sighed.

"The thing is, Rae-Rae felt really bad. Like she'd failed you."

"*Failed* me! She's the closest thing I've ever had to a friend." When I was silent Charity added, "I wish I could have explained to her."

"You still can," I said handing Charity my own phone. *Forgiveness is Rae-Rae's call to make.*

Charity scooted up on the bed, held my phone like it might dematerialize, thumbed and deleted for a long time. Finally she hit the "send" arrow. She started to hand my phone back to me but it pinged almost immediately. Charity looked at it, giggled, set it up where we could both hear, and hit play.

A squeaky-voiced Little Richard screamed, "Lucille! Please come back where you belong."

"I never got a chance to turn this in," I half-explained, forking over the safe phone Charity had left behind. After she was done texting back and forth with Rae-Rae, Charity looked . . . less sad. For such a tiny person, all her expressions were outsized.

"I *had* to run," she whispered.

I wasn't sure if she was talking to me or herself but I confirmed, "Sometimes it's the only way."

"They were going to send me home."

"To the people who *beat* you?" I know that happens but it still surprised me. She had looked pretty bad off the last day we'd seen her.

"No." Charity flicked her arm dismissively. "That was just some foster jerk who didn't like it that I refused to put out. I couldn't complain because then they really might send me home."

"And home is worse." I said it as a statement so it wouldn't sound like prying.

"Yes," Charity said, defensive. Paused, then added, "You wouldn't understand."

"Probably not," I conceded.

It wasn't the response she'd expected. She examined my face, trying to get a read.

"She's crazy." The words seemed to come out of Charity's mouth against her will. "My mother, she's crazy." And then Charity shut down.

What had Mrs. Meeny asked me? "Befriend her." How do I do that? I knew who would know but she wasn't here.

"Rae-Rae is great, isn't she? You picked good."

"I just got lucky finding someone so kind," Charity refused to take credit. Then, grateful to be on a less charged topic, she added, "And talented!"

"You mean her music?" I hadn't thought Rae-Rae sang or played an instrument except for fun.

Charity must not have either because she contradicted, "No, her art! I told her I like to draw and she texted me pics of some of her paintings. They're truly . . . vibrant. I could never create anything like that with color."

"She never showed them to me," I admitted.

I must have sounded wistful because Charity offered: "Would you like to see one of my drawings?"

She was in her room a long time—my guess was that she was sorting through them—and returned apologizing, "They're only pen and ink."

"Charity! You're a genius! Look at how detailed this is—I could stare at it for hours and still find something new! It's so simple but it has so much emotion!" I must have gone on like that for a long time because when I looked up at Charity she was blushing. She seemed really pleased.

"If I can only hang on for *four months* I'll be free. I'll find some kind of way to go to art school." Then she reverted to upset inside herself.

Talking to this girl sure has a lot of land mines. Tact is so not my strong point. Maybe I should just be blunt.

"Charity, you can tell me it's none of my business. But what happens in four months?"

"I turn eighteen. Then no one can send me back to her."

It would only sidetrack Charity to tell her she didn't look that old. Instead, I waited.

"My mother, I love her but she has a lot of . . . diagnoses. She'll be OK for a while and then something will happen, or she'll stop taking her medication, or sometimes it's straight out of the blue that one minute she's, well, my mom, and the next minute she's like not there. I don't know how to explain it."

"Charity, that must have been so hard for a kid to grow up with!"

"Sooner or later she goes off the rails. It gets obvious. Then they stick her in some institution. I get packed off to foster care temporarily but as soon as they decide she's 'stabilized' they 're-unite' us." Charity did air quotes to show her frustration.

I'd heard about "family reunification" before, how that was supposed to be an important goal of the family courts. Long ago I'd overheard my lawyer say that some people act as if it was the *only* goal but they were wrong. It had never occurred to me before to be grateful that there was no one to reunify me with.

" 'New girl.' That's what everyone always calls me. I've been in and out of dozens of schools which pretty much always means that I'm way behind everybody in my classes. It's not like I was going to *be* anyone anyway. But I've always loved to draw. Sometimes putting a pen to paper feels like the only thing that makes sense in my whole life."

"Charity"—I looked her in the eyes, wanting her to know this was important—"*they* don't get to decide who *we* are."

"I wish I could be as strong as you, Anna," Charity confessed sadly, "but when I'm around my mom too much I start to feel as crazy as she is. I'm afraid if I go back there this time, I'll be the one with a diagnosis and then I'll never get away."

"That's why you ran? Your mom was being released from the hospital and they were going to return you to her?"

"They'd *promised*. This last time when they sent me to foster care. They promised they would keep me in one place until I could graduate. I think they would have too, but that jerk, he didn't even bother to bruise me in places that wouldn't show. Once they had to take me out of there, they started making noises like that I'd be 'better off at home.'

"I planned it out ahead of time. I knew I didn't want to be on the street—that's dangerous!—but I'd heard about this place where a bunch of kids crash. I spent weeks stockpiling those little boxes of cereal they have here so I would have something to contribute when I got there. And the kids were pretty cool about it. No one bothered me. I wasn't even as hungry as I'd been in that foster home. Still, after a while . . . I really missed taking a shower. When I turned myself in and they brought me to the hospital, that's the first thing I did."

"That's why you're not in more trouble, Charity? Because you turned yourself in?"

"I'd always planned to. Running away, it's a crime. If you do it too often they lock you up, no matter if you had good reasons and you've done nothing wrong." *That's so unfair!* "I want a future, Anna. It's all I've ever wanted. Well, except the times when I didn't want anything at all."

"But aren't you afraid, now you're back, your mom will insist you come home?"

"If you ask for it, they have to give you a hearing." *That's true.* "And they're so slow, I'm hoping the four months will be up before they get around to me." *Well,* maybe *that's true too.* "I heard about asking for 'emancipation.' Like how the law can determine I'm an adult before my birthday. I'll be eighteen before that could get decided but at least it's another way to stall."

"Will they send you to another foster home?"

"God, I hope not!"

"Would it help if I spoke to the shelter manager for you? We get along pretty good."

"I don't know, Anna. It seems like asking for anything always gets you in trouble. I'd rather wait. But if they start talking about another placement, would you come with me and I'll talk to her?"

At least something *I could do.*

. . .

Over the next couple of days Charity and I talked more, but less intense. I told her about the shelter dogs while I shared my

Snickers bar. She promised me a picture for when I was back at the Good Farmers. *I definitely got the best of that deal.*

Going back to my regular life was on my mind though and I decided to talk it out with the one neutral person I could think of. When we had some private time I piled together all my resolve and then blurted out, "I need your help, Charity. I let down all my friends and I don't know how to make it right."

I told her about OBaaT. All of it, even the part that included her. I told her about Beemer and Willy's seizure and The Tsar letting Beemer return, and me disappearing on my friends because I couldn't face them. She asked for time to think it over. I was so ashamed I figured maybe she needed to decide if she wanted to hang out with me anymore.

When Charity got into my bed that night, she burrowed in like she had the first night. This time it was me who felt comforted.

"You've been thinking about this all wrong," Charity told me. "OBaaT is not yours with your friends helping *you* out. You have friends, Anna, good people. That's huge. Don't make it smaller. Each member of OBaaT signed on for themselves. The setbacks, they belong to all of you. And the only way to fight back is to fight back together."

That's what Ethan told us about attacking the mats.

While she'd been schooling me, I could hear in her voice the adult that Charity had been given no choice but to be for most of her life. But then the little kid peeked out: "I wish I'd had that," Charity regretted.

"You have Rae-Rae. And you have me. And you can have the others if you want them."

"See?" Charity smiled.

19

My mail slot at the Good Farmers was stuffed to the brim. I scooped it all on top of the pile of clean clothes I'd carried back from the shelter. *At least at the shelter I don't have to ask permission before using the machines.*

Back in my room with the door shut, I carefully sorted through.

Letters first. If there was bad news, I wanted to know about it. But there was nothing important except an announcement:

"To celebrate our tenth anniversary, this spring the Greene Street Shelter will be holding a festival in the park called RESCUES RULE! (date subject to park permit approval.) Invited as our guests are all the families of our adopted rescues and, of course, their rescued dogs. Please reach out to anyone you know who qualifies. Volunteers will also be needed for everything from food booths to setting up the obstacle course for an agility competition. Spread the word and, as always, thank you for being part of the Greene Street Family."

On my good days, I think maybe I am one of their rescues. I pinned the flyer to my bulletin board.

77

I set aside the one envelope with no return address.

There were seven handmade cards.

Sunny's card had a cartoon squirrel on the front. Pasted inside was a lacy Valentine cut out heart, with little sticker hearts all around it.

Rae-Rae's card front was a giant swirl painted in the brightest watercolors ever. Inside she'd used a broad black calligraphy pen on bright white paper to ink out eight musical notes holding each other's stems/hands. Eight?

The next card was a line drawing from Charity. That explained it. Rae-Rae had included her in this surprise and by extension into being one of the eight musical notes that were me and my friends. Charity must have worked like crazy to create one of her intricate edge-to-edge image collages in time to mail it off to me. After I'd opened the others I would look more closely but even at a glance it looked . . . less tightly drawn than the artwork she'd first shown me.

Piper's card was all glittery with gauzy pastel ribbon strips glued into a star shape. Inside, her beautiful penmanship read simply "I miss you." It looked lonely.

Jade had printed out a picture of Lilly-Belle and pasted it to the front of her card. Inside she'd sketched out an oval speech balloon that read "Arf! Arf! Arf! Arf! Arf!"

Tia's card was a precisely folded piece of typing paper with three unadorned words inside: "We need you."

Dareen's card had symbols on the front that I didn't understand. They looked sort of like a line drawing of waves with some random swells. Inside she'd translated, "Arabic for 'justice.' "

I set the cards aside and carefully slit open the plain envelope. I knew what it would say.

"01001001 00100000 01101100 01101111 01110110 01100101 00100000 01111001 01101111 01110101"

My techie had already taught me the binary code for "I love you."

. . .

As much as I dreaded facing my friends Monday—without those cards I don't know if I could have walked up the stairs to Dareen's apartment—the mood in the room was not at all what I had expected. No one wanted to hear my apologies or rehash really any of what had happened. Rae-Rae didn't even have a song for us. Tia summed it up, why we were here: "We need a plan."

And then I got it. "No," I disagreed, "we *have* a plan. Our mistake was to stop following it."

Charity was right. Making it ours instead of mine is more respectful.

"You mean the Beemer notebook?" Tia asked.

"No. I mean yes but only if it turns out the notebook is our best weapon." I knew I'd confused everyone so I started again. "Look, we hate bullies, right? I think we assumed that everybody does but they were too afraid to do anything. That was wrong. Beemer has . . . allies. Not only The Tsar and not because they're afraid of Beemer."

"Yes," Tia agreed, "that's why I nominated The Tsar at our first meeting. I think such people, they have—I don't know how to say it—common goals. They're not friends like we are. But protecting each other, they act as if it's in their self-interest."

"Like the cheerleading squad!" Piper interrupted. "No, don't you all look at me indulgently. This is important. The cheerleaders, they've tried to recruit me. They truly don't get it that I prefer my friends. Because for them, friendship doesn't mean that. Half the time, they don't seem to like each other. But they're joined to each other because for individual reasons cheerleading is precious to each of them—this is the part that matters—for their own *selfish* goals."

Jade nodded thoughtfully but then she shook something off in her head and didn't say anything, back to that force-shield around her.

Tia turned back to me: "How does that help us?"

"Beemer was gone for a week. I know that's not much but it means that The Tsar's protection only goes so far."

"If we can increase the pressure," Dareen jumped in, "sooner or later it will expose the points of vulnerability."

"Right!" I knew Dareen was speaking martial arts but it made sense.

"How do we increase pressure?" Tia wanted me to explain. Only partially Dareen's martial arts approach. Tia also wanted the rule to regain order.

"That's why I think what happened with Willy matters so much. As bad as that was, it was only one ugly incident. Maybe documenting a whole lot of ugliness—even if each one is not individually as bad—will have more effect." I rushed on, not wanting them disappointed that I was back to the notebook: "My suggestion is that we take one week, add as much as we can to the notebook, and then take it to my lawyer to see what she thinks. And if she thinks we're on the wrong track, maybe she'll have different suggestions. That's the best I've got," I finished off apologetically.

"No," Tia gaveled, "that's a direction."

Then she gave us her most beautiful and prophetic poem:

> OBaaT is a snow rose,
> grown in bitter cold,
> to flower defiance.

20

The way I got my lawyer, it was mostly by accident. I've been in a lot of "placements," which is what they call where they put you when you don't have a home of your own. The briefest one, I think I was about eight or nine. A caseworker was supposed to drop me off with a family that had a baby and two toddlers. By then I knew enough about foster care to get it that they wanted me as a babysitter.

When we got there, we could hear the little kids crying inside but it didn't seem like anyone else was home. The caseworker had to call the police to get the door unlocked. They didn't let me inside but even from the doorway—it smelled really bad. They sat me on the stoop outside while all these people came and went. After a while the caseworker came out and put me in her car to wait. Then I waited a bunch of other places until at the end of the day I was waiting in a courtroom.

There were some mean-looking people there who the judge called the "respondents." The judge was explaining that they had a new system in place called "one family/one judge." That meant that no matter what kind of hearing the family was in court for—he listed a bunch of different kinds—he would be their judge. They'd have the same lawyers appointed for each of them. Their children would each have their own same lawyers called "law guardians" appointed for them.

I didn't mean to but that's when I started to cry. I tried to be quiet about it.

Not right away but eventually the judge asked me why I was so upset. I apologized. He was kindly, which made me brave enough to ask him: "What if I don't have a family? Does that mean I can't have a lawyer?" I tried not to sound as sad as I felt.

"What is this child doing here?" the judge demanded of the audience.

The caseworker reluctantly answered: "Her status is long-term foster care."

"And?" The judge looked stern, but not at me.

"She was with me when . . ." The caseworker gestured toward the mean people, faltered weakly on: "I had nowhere else to put her. I've kept her with me while the agency tries to find a temporary placement."

"*That* was supposed to be her placement?" the judge demanded, glaring at the respondents.

The caseworker shrugged.

A now-angry judge scanned the people seated in the front row, pointed at a woman. "You're on the panel, right Ms. Horne?" She nodded. The judge asked my name, got some papers from his clerk, and wrote on them. While I watched, he signed them with a big flourish. That's all it took.

I remember the judge smiled quietly at me before he went back to work.

Later Ms. Horne explained that there's supposed to be a review of foster children but often the courts didn't get to it, or they did the review without the child being in the courtroom. "Now that I'm your lawyer I will make sure that your foster care progress will be reviewed annually by a judge with you right there to see it." She promised to stay on my case. I think she probably had to bend some rules to keep that promise. But she always has. And more.

That was a long time ago.

. . .

"Good work," my lawyer praised Tia and me after a silent 20 minutes of scanning through what we'd brought her. "I wish my investigators were this thorough."

"What's missing?" I asked. By then I knew Ms. Horne well enough that I wasn't diverted, although her words did make me proud.

"Well, the first thing that strikes me is that you talked to a lot of witnesses. That's the part investigators are most likely to overlook. But I'm not sure I understand why you haven't talked to any victims."

"We didn't want to make it worse," I admitted.

"Look Anna"—my lawyer hesitated—"I appreciate how mindful you are, you *all* are"—she nodded at Tia—"of people's privacy. But you also have to be respectful enough to give them a choice."

"What would that look like, Naomi?" Tia questioned.

"Ask, but be willing to accept 'no' for an answer." *OK. We could do that.* "You're at the investigative stage. That means information—all information—is a precious commodity. Once you've collected as much as you feel you can, then come back to me and we'll evaluate the strength of the information to determine what remedies might be available."

"Thank you." Tia thought we were done.

"You said 'the *first* thing'?" I prompted.

"Anna, you're a natural," my lawyer told me, making it sound like it was good I'd asked. "You're right that there is something else that seems . . . well, off and maybe significant. Are all of this Beemer person's victims male? How does he treat his female students?"

She's right! I snatched the notebook promising, "We'll find out."

21

New direction, new energy. Walking over to our next training session, Rae-Rae admonished us, Tommy Tucker style, to put on our "Hi-heel sneakers."

"Bring some boxing gloves," we all belted out in response, "in case some fool might wanna fight!"

By then Ethan was having us alternate who called out "Threat!" before we all grabbed defensive padding and attacked the mat. No matter who issued the warning, our movements and our reaction times were getting better.

Afterward, we sat with Ethan in our private space. It made sense to make him the first victimized person we interviewed.

"One observation," Ethan advised before we got started. "Talking to all of OBaaT at once could be intimidating. I know you all and trust you but for anyone else, it could feel claustrophobic, or worse."

"Good point," Sunny squeezed in her reassurance before Tia or the rest of us could respond. She smiled at Ethan as if only the two of them truly understood each other.

"We'll organize assignments before we leave today," Tia orchestrated. "But is it comfortable for you to talk with all of us now?"

Ethan hesitated, swallowing a lump in his throat before he braved the words, "If it's not presumptuous, I've come to feel like I *am* one of you."

Charity taught me this. I walked over to Ethan—I had to hip-bump Sunny out of the way to do it—held out my hand, shook his. One by one so did everyone else.

"But you're still not invited to Dareen's," Tia clarified, making us laugh at her "point of procedure." *Everyone* knew Dareen's grandmother's rule: "No strangers." Proving in was a long process. I'm not sure guys could qualify.

"Could I do this as a narrative?" Ethan asked, sounding even more academic because he had something difficult to talk about.

"Questions at the end," Tia agreed.

"For a long time Beemer was indifferent to me. After a while, I felt him watching my interactions with classmates, studying me with a cold contempt emanating from his very being." *Ethan's words get bigger and bigger the more uncomfortable he is.* "I should have had the self-discipline not to react to his scorn but it was painful—"

"—Self-blame is not allowed," Tia corrected.

"Yes." Ethan reorganized his thoughts. "I did blame myself—which increased the pain exponentially. I've already listed as many of the specific statements he made as I can"—we nodded—"but the words by themselves don't convey the harm. It's like his hatred was wielded as if it were a penetrating weapon.

The most disconcerting experience, though, was when it suddenly stopped. Beemer seemed to revert to indifference without any precipitating event. I've tried to trace back to a moment when his torment altered. I can't identify a point. More like a period of time. When I started working with you all. When Sunny and I started seeing each other."

"And *being* seen," I said, more to myself than to OBaaT.

"Oh goodness, that's right!" Sunny made it a group conversation. "The first time Beemer saw Ethan and me holding hands, I could *feel* him staring. For a while after that, it was like he was studying the two of us. And then, as Ethan said, it was like he lost interest in us entirely."

"It *can't* be that he knows about OBaaT," Jade actually volunteered. "Yes, he intervened when Anna announced the I-Hate-Bullies club but it feels like we've all been off his radar since. And if he did know about OBaaT, how would he also know that Ethan was with us?"

"Anna's lawyer"—Tia invoked the title to give it more authority—"noticed that none of the victims in the notebook are girls. Do you think this is all—that term I hate—'homosexual panic'? He thought Ethan was gay until he saw him with Sunny?"

"Nothing about Beemer's bullying seems like panic to me," Dareen objected. "It feels . . ."

"Intentional, malicious," Ethan filled in, agreeing. "Why do you hate that term, Tia?"

"Why does it only ever get applied to males? And what makes it an excuse to be vicious? Plenty of people are afraid to be gay."

"Besides," Dareen got us back on track, "there's plenty of non-gay kids in our notebook. Like Willy. Nobody's ever thought he was gay. Only . . . different."

"You're right." Tia nodded to herself. "I don't even think he's a bigot."

"Even with all the awful things he says to Hispanics?" Sunny asked, looking to Ethan for an explanation.

"You're saying that Beemer is a sadist, pure and simple, right Tia? That what all us targets have in common is some perceived vulnerability—*whatever* that might be."

Tia looked surprised to hear that's what she'd meant but she didn't disagree. Ethan's words sounded so true.

"I've been trying to figure out Beemer's deal about girls," I said, out loud this time. "The only personal thing he ever says to us is 'See me after school.' "

"That's right!" Dareen agreed. "He did that to me once but all he did was ask me about my sister. Like were we really related? When I said 'yes' he dismissed me without ever saying why he'd asked to see me. What about the rest of you?"

"I told him I couldn't because I had to be at the dojo." Tia.

"I told him my father was picking me up." After a pause Piper added, "Beemer spooked me when he contradicted what I'd said: 'I thought you lived with your mother,' but he dropped the whole topic when I answered 'joint custody.' "

"He never asked me." Sunny.

"Or me, either." Jade.

"I said 'no'." Rae-Rae. That made us laugh because . . . naturally she did. Rae-Rae doesn't offer excuses.

"I told him I had an appointment with my lawyer." I finished it.

"Experimental probes," Ethan described them. He looked like the words tasted bad in his mouth.

"Explain?" Tia sounded more thoughtful than confused.

"All of his requests were pretextual, right?" Ethan continued without waiting for us to answer: "He never followed up because the *only* reason he asks to see girls after school is to find out which ones are vulnerable. I'd venture to guess he's checked everyone's school records looking to see who might be manipulated because of their background or homelife. Then he tests to see who has support systems that aren't self-evident in the records."

"For what?" I asked, not sure I wanted to hear the answer.

"It's grooming!" Jade responded. "Ethan and I, you too Piper, we were all in that Health Education class. The one where that teacher talked to us like adults with brains—"

"—No wonder they canceled it after that one term," Rae-Rae interrupted. "I really wanted to take that."

"Anyway," Jade continued, "pedophiles—"

"—*predatory* pedophiles," Ethan corrected. "That's what our Health Education teacher told us, remember: 'Pedophile' describes how someone feels. 'Predatory pedophile' refers to what they do. The articles he had us read said that their first step is to narrow down the field of potential victims to the ones most likely to be easy prey."

"Are we saying we think Beemer is a *rapist*?" I blurted out.

"I think we should bring in your techie, Anna," was Ethan's only response.

Although we were distracted by then, Tia wouldn't let us adjourn without our interview assignments. She divided our notebook victims into categories. She made a sign-up sheet for us to fill in our names.

LGBTQ

Tia, Rae-Rae, Anna

UNPOPULAR

Piper, Sunny, Dareen

SPEECH IMPAIRED

Ethan, Sunny, Anna

ESL

Jade, Dareen, Tia

When we'd gotten to English as a Second Language, there'd been a pause. Rae-Rae filled it with: "I wish they'd let Charity have a day pass from the teen shelter. She speaks perfect Spanish."

Another thing I didn't know about Charity. Noisy as she is, Rae-Rae is so much better at listening.

Finally Jade reluctantly volunteered, "Spanish was all I spoke until I was four."

Not that she looked less shielded, but Jade had talked more today than she had in months. No one wanted to break the spell by asking any questions. Dareen offered to help Jade with interviewing Spanish kids if Jade would help her with other languages. Tia agreed to be their third.

Now all I had to worry about was that Piper had barely spoken in the meeting. And that I would have to talk with my Hoke about OBaaT. And that it was starting to look like we were all in way over our heads.

22

As beautiful as he was, this new Greene Street dog, Polar Bear, was a handful. A huge Great Pyrenees mix—you know, those blue-white mountain dogs, all fur and muscle, no fat, no give— who wanted me to understand I was *his* sheep. We'd only gone a few streets on our walk when he dragged me over to a sad heap of clothing that turned out to be . . . Jade. She was hunched down hugging her knees. Polar Bear announced his unequivocal intention to stay splayed over her, guarding her with his life until whatever enemy had done this was vanquished. I don't know if it was recognizing the depth of Jade's sadness or the brick wall of Polar Bear's obstinance but I sat down beside them on the sidewalk.

"Is it your little Lilly-Belle?" I asked, worried for the old dog. Last time I'd bumped into them, Lilly-Belle had looked healthy for her age but sometimes it's hard for me to tell. I'd seen them a lot together. Jade would always be talking to Lilly-Belle as she walked her, the two of them perfect company for each other. My guess was Jade told the dog her troubles. I made it a point not to eavesdrop but even from a distance I could see Lilly-Belle was a

92

good listener. My friend had my complete sympathy at the idea she might lose Lilly-Belle.

Jade totally sidetracked my thoughts by answering, "I ought to be happy for her." A tear dripped out of her eye and Polar Bear won my heart forever by tonguing it off.

"Jade?"

"There's a social work student who volunteers here at the shelter." Jade took in a trembling breath then told the whole story at once to get it over with: "She has a part-time job caring for a woman resident at an assisted living facility. The resident loves dogs and misses hers. The facility allows dogs as long as there's someone to walk, water, and feed the animal. This social work student, she worked it all out that she'll be the one to do that. Now she's testing out Greene Street dogs to see which one to choose. Today she took Lilly-Belle."

"Oh Jade, you don't know that Lilly-Belle will get chosen!"

"Lilly-Belle *is* the best. You know her. Lilly-Belle is the best dog ever."

"Listen to me, Jade. Adoption doesn't work like that." *Don't be hurt. She didn't mean it about you.* "It's not who's best. It's who's the best fit." *How many times has some worker repeated those supposed-to-comfort words to me?* "Maybe they're looking for a younger dog, or the resident wants one that reminds her of the dog she used to have or . . . You know what? The people in Greene Street, they might just decide to pick the dog that needs it the most. Because of you, Lilly-Belle is the happiest dog in the place."

Jade looked slightly less forlorn. Since Polar Bear was now determined to lie next to her for the foreseeable future, I continued. "If it *is* her they pick though, you're going to have a hard decision." Totally unaware she was doing it, Jade leaned her head on Polar Bear who emitted a contended rumble and fluffs of excess fur as she patted his neck. "You have to choose. Do you ask the social work student if you can still walk Lilly-Belle sometimes? Or do you start walking a new dog?"

"I love her," Jade whispered, "and sh-she loves me. It hurts to think about not ever seeing her again."

"Then that's your decision," I told her, trying to keep disappointment out of my voice. "We'll ask Greene Street as soon as we get back, just in case Lilly-Belle is picked."

"But," Jade continued as if I hadn't spoken, "if I love her then I have to want the best life for her. Polar Bear, what do you think?" She looked at his large furry face as if he had an answer. Then she nodded to herself. "Yes, let's ask the shelter!" She turned to me: "It doesn't have to be a choice—I could do both. Lilly-Belle probably wouldn't need daily walks. It could be less often as long as we don't lose each other. And you're right, other dogs need me too."

Had I said that out loud? I had tried so hard not to.

"Polar Bear!" but he was not going anywhere without Jade. As soon as she agreed to walk with us the Great Pyr proudly tail-waved us down the street. *Yes, Polar Bear, that tail is as magnificent as you think it is.*

23

The discussion with my Hoke—the one I'd promised OBaaT—
was weighing on me. So far I had avoided it on the pretense that
I needed to think it through first. I should get over this delusion
that I'm good at not showing how I feel. Apparently I'm pretty
transparent.

"Anna, what's on your mind?" my Hoke asked me gently. We
were walking in that new part of town with all the construction.
It always surprises me that totally public places are the most
private.

I recapped the last meeting for my techie, ending with
Ethan's suggestion.

My Hoke examined my face intensely. "Do you want my help,
or are you inviting me to join OBaaT?"

"We need your help, Hoke," I answered.

"To be your techie?"

"Yes."

"Then, no."

"Just 'no'?" I couldn't believe it.

"Just 'no,' " he confirmed.

We never argued. I wasn't going to start now when I was this hurt. I turned away to walk off alone—the way I guessed I was.

"You *always* want to be alone," Hoke shouted after me as if he could read my thoughts. "You push everyone away. You never let anyone in."

"Because this is what happens when I do." I'd turned back to answer his shouting with my own. It felt as if the breakable parts of me were splintering open.

Hoke stopped shouting but he was no less angry. "Do you have any idea how insulting it is that you only want my tech skills? I let you call me your techie because it made you smile. But being a techie is something I do, not who I am."

"I'm sorry," I said, meaning it. "I'll never call you my techie again."

He wasn't done. "I would have been proud and happy if you'd asked me to join OBaaT," Hoke admitted, so sorrowfully that I couldn't stand it. "Don't you think there's someone fouling the air at every school? That there are bullies everywhere? That I don't hate them all? That I don't know personally that kids like us are favorite targets? Did you really think this wasn't my battle too?"

"I knew you understood, Hoke—"

"—but I'm not good enough to be with you, only useful for some 'skills'?" he pronounced bitterly.

"*That's* why you said 'no'?" I gasped. "Listen Hoke, you have to believe me. The reason I chose asking only for your tech help is because I thought if I picked the other choice, joining OBaaT, it would be asking too much."

"It never occurred to you that should be my decision?"

I had that coming.

"Don't push me away, Anna."

That means I'm forgiven.

. . .

The next afternoon at Dareen's I made a point of waiting until everyone was done studying before I said anything. This was going to take a while.

When I got to the part about why I wasn't going to call Hoke my techie anymore Tia mercifully deflected the conversation.

"Guys make everything complicated," she observed wryly, half-serious. It meant a lot to me that Tia trusted us enough to say that.

Piper said "Amen" a little too quickly at the same time that Sunny snorted, "Oh yeah, like women are *always* straightforward."

I worried what—or more likely which one of us—was on Sunny's mind but this conversation was a whole lot easier than recapping my argument with Hoke. "It felt so right yesterday shaking Ethan's hand, like . . . ratifying he was one of us. But now with Hoke, well OBaaT is not only us anymore."

"It's not like OBaaT is turning into a couples thing," Tia observed. "Two people willing to fight alongside us, they're allies. We should honor that." Dareen nodded, getting it about combat.

"*This*," Rae-Rae insisted, spreading her arms to include the room, "is *us*. OBaaT is something we're part of and it can expand to include people who are with us. But it doesn't change *us*."

"Rae-Rae, don't go all Sister Sledge on us," Tia interrupted. *She must think this conversation is too raw, waving that red flag of disco in Rae-Rae's face.*

For once Rae-Rae was too serious to be sidetracked. "That's not music, let alone wisdom. The blues is the only truth. I've taught you all about rock and roll because it's teenage blues. But some blues is universal." As she'd talked she'd been swiping through her phone. "You all need to hear this. It's Lightnin Hopkins: 'Walking this Road by Myself.' The one where Billy Bizor accompanies him."

She played a song that was so piercingly lonely I almost couldn't bear to listen. When it was done Rae-Rae stared at each of us to make sure we were paying attention. "That's not any of us." When we all nodded Rae-Rae backed off of it: "The funny thing is, it isn't them either. That singer and that harp, that was a *conversation*." (I was proud I remembered that "harp" meant harmonica.) "Now we need to have a conversation of our own."

We did and then Tia ended with a new poem:

> War warriors,
> double-stranded pearls
> of forever family.

24

Hoke didn't want to "disrupt the pattern" of our training sessions. Dareen's place was obviously out of the question. Despite their objections, it was Sunny's parents who allowed us to meet there. Why did it not surprise me that their home smelled like baking.

After Sunny's mom and dad disappeared to give us privacy, I introduced Hoke. I was too concentrated on doing it right to acknowledge my friends' happiness at finally meeting him. I absorbed it though, enough to give me the strength to say: "Hoke is not my techie. He is my boyfriend. But what's more important, he is my friend and *our* friend if you want him to be. No matter your choice, he is on our side."

When I had the courage to glance sideways at Hoke he looked embarrassed and proud at the same time.

Even more formal than usual because he was unsure of himself, Ethan apologized as if the wrong was his: "I'm sorry to have worded it inappropriately at our last session, asking Anna for her techie's help. We are grateful to have you join us." Ethan paused for what he would call "verification" and then continued. "I hope it is not offensive that we also need your techno-logical assistance."

"About that." Hoke rolled his eyes, relaxing all of us with hu-mor. "There's skills and then there's the right skills. If you need coding, I'm your man. From what I can tell though, you need an expert in internet investigations." Hoke veered the topic: "Like social media to start with. Besides the OBaaT Facebook page I created—that none of you are maintaining—are any of you ac-tive online?"

"We're keeping the OBaaT page for when we need it," I mum-bled weakly.

"Not counting Instagram and Snapchat for the usual stuff, do you have individual FB accounts? Twitter?" Hoke listed a bunch of other names we'd barely heard of.

We shook our heads "no" or made faces. When he mentioned posting photos, Piper literally crossed her index fingers in front of her in a "warding off evil" gesture that looked . . . serious. "We don't have time!" Rae-Rae answered for all of us, covering for Piper. "And besides, going viral as a life's goal is so pathetic."

Hoke tried one more time although it was obvious he already knew the answer: "None of you are into gaming? chatrooms? nothing where you interact with strangers?"

Resigned, Hoke agreed to some small part of what he thought we needed: "Look, I'll do the best I can searching the basic plat-forms to see what accounts Beemer has and then I'll look for someone who might have insider knowledge how to penetrate those accounts."

"What is it we're looking for?" Tia asked Ethan because this had been his idea.

Ethan chilled us with the words: "If Beemer's contacts with females are surreptitious, then there's a high probability he's reaching out online."

Tia called it, getting us back to work we knew how to do: "In the meantime we'll see what we can find out about what Beemer's been doing up close and personal."

Tia handed Hoke our notebook in what felt like a ceremonial gesture. We were silent while he studied it. I spent the time catching up with myself.

"Are these categories written in stone?" Hoke looked up from our chart to ask us after he'd added his name next to "unpopular."

"You think we've missed something?" Tia sounded attentive, not defensive. *I wish I had her self-confidence.*

"What about physical appearance?" Hoke thought it through out loud: "I mean I know it probably overlaps with categories we already have." *I love him saying 'we.'* "But doesn't Beemer target some kids because they're fat or have a deformity or . . . ?"

"Yes!" Piper agreed quickly. "He, like, favors that too-smooth, preppy look. Anything else he *judges*. You can see it."

"Not only judges—targets," Tia reminded her.

"The kids in your category, they're going to be hard to talk to," I cautioned, remembering before I had known Ethan when I'd tried reaching out to anyone who seemed lonely like me. It had dead-ended.

"To be candid"—Ethan hesitated—"I think it would be best if Hoke and I took that category."

"Why?" Tia wanted to know.

"It might be mortifying for a male interview subject to be asked if Beemer targeted their, um, attributes."

Hoke nodded gratefully.

"Besides"—Ethan blushed—"you're all too pretty."

We booed him. From anyone else those words would have sounded patronizing. Even from Ethan … but Sunny cut through the tension by commenting, "Well, you two are too pretty too."

Then of course Rae-Rae couldn't resist singing: "I ain't saying you ain't pretty." *Linda Ronstadt: "Different Drum."*

We'd had enough for one meeting anyway.

25

Rae-Rae and I finally got permission to visit Charity at the teen shelter. Rae-Rae brought so huge a portfolio of her paintings that I worried I'd be left out of the sharing between two artists. Turns out, being an appreciative audience is, well, appreciated.

"Guess what!" Charity said, not able to hold on to her news any longer. "When the normal staff came back after the holidays they assigned me this incredibly cool woman. She was only here for a month longer but she's into art herself. When she saw me working on my graphics she brought me these"—Charity gestured toward two new sketchpads—"and these!" Charity waved a drawing pencil set. "And"—she took in an extra breath for the real announcement: "She helped me apply to art school! She found a 'Promising Young Artists' college program in Chicago where I might be able to go once I get my GED. Returning to regular high school doesn't make sense but I've already started to study for my equivalency diploma."

Chicago! Far away!

"Best news ever!" Rae-Rae said, so unselfishly that I felt it too.

Rae-Rae sang "Turn Me Loose" while we danced around. "Doc Pomus, the songs he wrote could make even a glutz like Fabian a chart-topper."

After we'd celebrated with the cookies Sunny had baked and sent along, Charity wanted to know all our news. Of course we filled her in about OBaaT but she also wanted the latest on all the shelter dogs. Charity is like me and I guess Jade. Having our own dogs is never going to be part of our lives until we're on our own.

"You will never believe it," I told her, excited. "They found the right family for Rocky the Raucous! The shelter told me those folks have so many energetic kids, when they try hard enough they can wear Rocky out. I'm not sure I believe it myself but it does seem like this time his adoption is really going to stick." It made me a peaceful kind of happy to picture the Rottweiler mix finally having the home he'd dreamed of.

Charity asked me about Lilly-Belle and I filled her in about Jade's dilemma. It occurred to me that Jade wanting Lilly-Belle to have her happiness was a lot like how I felt about Charity going to Chicago. I updated Charity with the rest of the news: "And Jade was right. They did want her Lilly-Belle for the assisted living resident. But they've worked it out. Sunday mornings while the woman and her assistant go to church, Jade spends a few hours just her and Lilly-Belle."

"Is Jade walking other dogs too?" Rae-Rae asked. I already knew I wasn't the only one who worried about Jade.

"I'm trying to talk her into Polar Bear." I explained who he was. "But at least for now she only walks the little ones."

"Polar Bear is a protector?" Charity asked.

I guess Rae-Rae and I really have told Charity all about all of us. Even locked away in here and never having met our friends or the shelter dogs, Charity just seemed to get it.

"He is!" I bragged. "It's in his nature. But being in a shelter has also made him a worry-dog. He puts up a good front but something is eating at his heart."

"You know who Polar Bear belongs with?" Rae-Rae answered herself: "Piper! They are both gorgeous and haunted."

"Is she still hiding inside herself?" Charity asked.

"Jade?" I thought we were still talking about Lilly-Belle. "She's lowered her barrier about an inch," I answered.

Rae-Rae smiled sadly before turning to Charity: "I thought you meant Piper."

"Piper *is* acting different, isn't she?" I mulled it over: "She hasn't mentioned her boyfriend Lance in like forever but still, it's as if he's dimmed her somehow."

"I'm sorry, Charity," Rae-Rae apologized. "This must be hard to follow. We have two friends who we don't know how to help."

I tried to explain: "Jade, it's like she's closed herself against the world and only Lilly-Belle is allowed in. Piper has always been open but something is seeping into her, stealing her from us."

Charity said mostly to herself, "I understand how shadows can take over."

"I'm worried about both of them," I admitted.

"Does Jade have a new shelter favorite?" Charity asked. She was right, there was no point analyzing problems we didn't know how to fix.

"Well, it's definitely not Thug," I laughed, "but he's going to a breed rescue for Cocker Spaniels anyway. Greene Street is good at recognizing the dominant breed in a mutt and then reaching out to the rescue groups that specialize in them. And only a Cocker Spaniel lover will truly appreciate Thug's . . . spirit.

"The other day they brought in a new sad little thing that I think would be perfect for Jade. He doesn't look like much, you'd barely notice him, but as soon as you show him any kindness he runs right over and hugs you. No, really, he puts his front legs around whatever part of you he can reach and squeezes! Who could resist that?"

"You all take such good care of each other," Charity praised us, "and me. I'm sorry I'm useless. If I do get to escape to Chicago, my only second thoughts are that I won't ever have done anything to reciprocate."

"Be serious!" Rae-Rae objected. "Without you, there would be no OBaaT."

"You're the one who made us believe that what we do could matter," I seconded Rae-Rae.

26

This first victim interview was not going well.

"Newsflash," Derrick (*I doubt that's his real name*) condescended, "Beemer hates us because we're ho-mo-sex-u-als. So do lots of people. You'd know that," he spit at Tia, "if you—"

"—I get it," Rae-Rae met him scorn-for-scorn. "You all loud and proud. But that's a choice. One choice. Not everyone wants to come out to everybody all the time to earn their gay badge. That don't mean they're in the closet."

"B—" Derrick started.

A quiet kid in the corner cut him off: "—Derrick is right." He spoke with dignity: "We face a lot of discrimination. But you're right too. It's different with Beemer."

"How?" My first contribution of the night, limited to one word.

"He makes it *personal*," a third kid added. *I hope Tia is tracking who is who.* "It's not like 'I hate homosexuals.' It's like 'I hate *you*. You personally. You disgust me.'"

"And he turns it on and off for his audience," said a different voice. "If no one's around he'll ignore me. But if his groupies can hear, he wants to cheerlead the hate."

"The worst part is, some of the taunters, we *know* they're gay."

"But that's not Tia," Rae-Rae countered.

They must have silently confirmed that truth because suddenly they were all talking at once.

"He giggled that if I ever got arrested, I'd have a *good* time in jail."

"On Ash Wednesday he told me to scrub my forehead because God hated my kind."

"He pointed me out to a whole sixth-grade class that came to tour the high school, warning them to stay away from me and anyone like me."

On and on. When they'd run down, I questioned, "Have you witnessed him bullying kids who don't seem gay?" and when they acknowledged they had: "Do you think he's worse to you?"

They did, but that was hard for me to evaluate. Everyone feels their own pain most. Beemer, I was getting convinced he picked on any easy target—like what mattered was the power, not the reason.

Rae-Rae and Tia wanted to know what they'd witnessed.

"Mostly he leaves the black kids alone. I think he's scared of them."

"The Spanish kids, he likes to Trump-taunt them about what will happen 'when the real president gets back.' "

"As fat as he is, he still makes fun of kids' bodies."

I asked about Willy. They all got quiet. Everyone knew: Willy was Beemer at his worst.

"Can I help???" I'd texted Hoke but he hadn't answered.

Something was wrong. He'd blind-marched into the Good Farmers' late and sweaty, asked to take an off-schedule shower, and then withdrew into his room. I was in no position to object to someone wanting to be left alone.

After what seemed like forever, he texted back, "#BeamOnBeemer."

When I texted back a question mark his answer was simply, "tomorrow."

. . .

"I had an idea"—Hoke shook his head—"but it's probably stupid."

Hoke is never stupid and it wasn't an idea that had him this upset. When I'd shown up at his school right after classes he'd seemed . . . someplace else. An angry someplace else.

"I was headed off to the gym," Hoke explained, "to hit the punching bag again. Not that it did any good yesterday."

"What happened?" I asked him gently.

"Ethan and I interviewed a kid." Hoke tried to sound neutral but failed. Whatever he was looking at in his memory, it had maggots on it.

"That awful?"

Hoke turned toward me. His eyes gentled as he traced the outline of my cheek with his fingers. "Yes." He forced himself into get-to-work mode. "We'll write it up for the notebook but . . ."

"You should tell me too?"

"Yes, Anna."

I told him I was ready.

"The kid uses a wheelchair. I don't know why but it wasn't recent and it didn't seem temporary. I thought he got around pretty good but he didn't think so."

"Beemer's doing?" I prompted when Hoke paused for too long.

"The wheelchair, there's nothing wrong with it. But when the kid got transferred into Beemer's class, the first day the kid wheeled himself in Beemer stopped mid-sentence, held his hand up to his ear, and turned to the kid in mock concern. 'Doesn't that noise drive you crazy?' Beemer asked him that first time. When the kid tried to answer that he didn't hear anything unusual, Beemer demanded of his toadies, 'Don't you all hear a *squeak*?' On the spot, Beemer started calling the kid 'Squeaky.'

"It's so bad, Anna, that's what the kid calls *himself* now, how he introduced himself to Ethan and me . . ." Hoke paused again but this time I allowed him to continue if/when he was ready.

"The next day, Beemer had a spray can that said WD-40. He offered it to the kid, made rusty wheel noises, waited for his brown-nosers' contempt when the kid couldn't reach around to the wheel Beemer was telling him to fix. Beemer gaslighted the kid with that oilcan for *months*, convincing him he was crazy if he didn't hear that squeak. Every day. Every day. Every single day . . ."

Hoke and I, we know what it feels like to be poisoned from the inside.

"It ate into the kid, Anna. Ethan and I could see it. But we couldn't stop it."

For a long time afterward I thought about Hoke's fingers touching my cheek, how it felt like love and sadness at the same time, like I was the only sweet-smelling thing on a rancid planet.

27

Ethan and Sunny and I had spent a couple of afternoons on a bench near the Speech Pathology Clinic but none of the students we recognized were willing to talk to us.

While we were waiting I asked Ethan what gaslighting really was. He did that thing where he nods to himself before answering. Ethan knows me, so first he verified, "You're not using the colloquialism, right? The way people throw around the term any time someone disagrees with them?"

I knew Hoke would only use a word scientifically so, no. "Like with Squeaky," I clarified.

Ethan flickered that same sorrow I'd seen in Hoke but forced himself past it to ask: "You already researched the dictionary definition?"

"To cause a person to doubt his or her sanity through the use of psychological manipulation," I repeated what I'd memorized.

"That definition, everybody knows now it comes from an old movie called 'Gaslight' where a husband convinced his wife she was crazy. But it seems to me the concept is more complicated than movie truth, more like convincing a victim that they are insane *unless* they accept the abuser's fraudulent version of reality. It's like insisting that the victim trust the gaslighter more than they trust themselves. A pure power rush for a bully." Ethan looked to me to see if I was following. I started to ask more but some huge friendly guy was all of a sudden shaking Ethan's hand almost off his arm.

"You're Ethan, right?" the guy swarmed him. "You're Gabriel's younger brother! I'm Terrence. No reason you should remember me, but Gabriel, he was the only reason I survived high school."

"Terrence?" Ethan managed to mumble. "But—"

"I know. I know. I probably didn't say one word to you when you met me. I used to have a really bad stutter. Gabriel, he was the only one who treated me like I was human. He always acknowledged me, even if it was only a nod in my direction. He always let me finish a sentence no matter how long it took. You have no idea how many people don't do that. Rude people interrupt but the others, they think it's being kind to speak our words for us."

Sunny's eyes had been getting bigger and bigger until the question popped out of her: "But you don't stutter at all now."

"Kind of you to say!" Terrence answered Sunny, nodded approval of her to Ethan, then turned to all of us, so that keeping up with him was like watching the Ping-Pong table at the teen shelter. "But it's not totally gone. I still have to concentrate if I feel too intense about something. This place though"—he tilted his head toward the Speech Pathology Clinic—"you can't imagine how much they've helped me. I still come here for myself when I need it but mostly I'm here as a mentor for younger kids."

Terrence slowed his roll before looking at me quietly and questioningly. Speaking would answer his question so I asked mine: "You stopped talking much?"

"It was really bad when I was in high school. There was this evil cretin of a teacher who made me want to check out entirely. *Beemer!* He would repeat every syllable I stuttered, draw it out until his trolls laughed at me. I *hated* him. But my hatred only inspired his cruelty. I couldn't stop him. I did the only thing I could do. I stopped talking period. Do you know how lonely that is? Lots of times I would think about how it would be easier, better to be dead. Like I said, it was bad."

"How did Gabe help?" Ethan wanted to know.

"That's hard to explain," the guy who now had more words than anybody answered. "I think when people are suicidal, somewhere inside they really want to believe that the world is not as bleak as it feels. I had no evidence of that except your brother. But he was somehow enough. The Tsar—do you still call him that?—he was new then. Once I stopped talking I think he was afraid that teacher, Beemer"—*He stuttered on* B—"his name was, had gone too far. That's my guess why they let me graduate with the rest of my class. When I'd been away from all that . . . toxicity for long enough, I came here. The Speech Pathology Clinic gave me my life back."

"I think you *took* it back," Sunny praised him.

"Good for you," Terrence told Ethan pointing his head at Sunny. Then doing that ping-pong thing again, he turned to all of us: "What are you all doing hanging around this building?"

We explained. As talkative as Terrence was, he heard us out. Then he said, "I don't know if any of the students here are ready to talk about Beemer." *There it is again, he stutters on that name.* "I'll ask them for you if you want. But regardless, if you reach the point that you need someone to sign a statement or testify"—Terrence started looking frightened but he forced himself to finish the sentence—"I will."

"I am very proud to have met you." I hoped my words conveyed even a fraction of how I felt.

"Likewise," Terrence told all of us.

28

We were all supposed to report in about our interviews on Saturday at Sunny's. Thursday afternoon, I got called down to the language arts room. Again. I hadn't had a private conversation with Mrs. Harbinger since before OBaaT.

She looked nervous when she handed me a slip of paper. Handwritten on it was a name, "Colton Bridgeway," a title, "Adams County District School Board Member," and a phone number with the word "cell" in parenthesis after it.

"This may be a resource," Mrs. Harbinger said. It sounded deliberately oblique.

"How did you know—" I started to ask her.

"—The walls have ears." She shrugged.

I couldn't tell if that was an answer or a warning. I guessed it could be both. "Thank you," I settled for, looking her straight in the eye for the first time in months. Not that I forgave her but I appreciated that giving me the note cost her a lot.

29

Our "unpopular" category and Hoke's "physical appearance" category and the new one those two had invented called the "bad at sports" group had so many overlaps that Ethan and Hoke took all of them. The rest of us tried to track down rumors, looking to talk to any girls that Beemer showed special interest in. The first part was easy—there were tons of rumors. But the second part was impossible—none of those girls had anything to say to us and resented us asking. The closest we came was someone who'd transferred to a different school. She looked really upset when we brought up Beemer's name but all she would tell us is that she'd "better not" talk to us.

Berry was the exception. She definitely had a lot to say. She stopped me on my way to my last class on Friday, stormed right up to me, face all red and her whole body shaking with un-righteous indignation. She poked her finger at my breastbone. "Leave him alone."

"I don't—"

"—Don't try to deny it." Still poking. "Frederick Beemer"—*Frederick?*—"is the best teacher in this school. You don't deserve him. You and your little pals better stop trying to make trouble for him. You—"

"—Get your hands off of me."

"Or what?" She raised her voice, scorned, "Or you'll go to the *principal*? Lots of luck with that strategy."

I pulled out my cell, hit record, held it toward Berry. "Do you want to repeat what you just said?" I challenged.

"I sure do—" Berry started then interrupted herself, sneering. "Oh, your posse."

I was so focused on Berry it didn't register until I replayed that word in my head. *Behind me. Jade. Dareen. Tia. Piper. Rae-Rae. Sunny. My friends had stepped up one by one.*

"You'll be alone sometime," Berry threatened before stomping away.

For some reason, it reminded me of Piper's boyfriend Lance. His special knock: "You are Mine."

30

By ten Saturday morning when we got there, Sunny's parents had already left their house "for the afternoon." A note on the fridge told us to call for pizza if we got hungry. Sunny told us the number they had left belonged to a takeout place where they had a family account. We could order whatever we wanted. We didn't though. It wasn't that kind of day.

We compared notes about Berry, Mrs. Harbinger, the interview results from the ESL interviews. Dareen hadn't found any Arabic kids willing to talk to her. I think she scared them. The Asian kids, she told us, all conceded Beemer was a total racist but the way it worked out for them, he mostly left them alone. Dareen read from her notes: "He thinks we're all geniuses. Like he's afraid we'll turn him in to the Spelling Bee police or something."

Tia looked like she wanted to add something but didn't want to interrupt Dareen. I asked and she kind of sighed before observing, "The Asian girls, they had like almost a cringe whenever anyone mentioned Beemer's name. The Asian guys, they were more contemptuous."

We didn't know what to do with that information. Dareen continued with her report. The Asian kids agreed with what the LBGTQs had told us: Beemer left the black kids alone. He seemed physically afraid of them like they were all murderous gangbangers. Dareen thought the Spanish kids were only half-joking when they muttered they wished Beemer knew enough about Central American gangs to fear them too.

Jade told us some of the vile threats Beemer had made to the Spanish kids. Mean and cruel and ugly. Still, there was one light moment when Jade confided, "They call Beemer *cecílido*." She laughed: "I looked it up and the English name is 'caecilian.' " We still looked blank. Jade explained, "It's a blind, legless snake that looks a lot like a worm. That's the polite description but I think they meant the obscene one."

"A penis snake," Tia filled in drily. Somehow the way she said it so matter-of-factly made it funnier. We all wanted Jade to teach us how to say the word and repeated "say-see-lee-doe" until we got it right.

We compiled the reports into our notebook. After our sessions Hoke had been inputting each report and converting it into a pdf to share it more easily. We all agreed I should talk to my lawyer ASAP. Piper asked if she could come along this time. Sure. *Why?*

We were pretty down by then. Beemer's viciousness, it made us sick. All the different kinds of hate concentrated together sapped our strength. Although it was early we were about to call it a day when Sunny asked if she could say something.

"People think I'm *nice*." She made a bad-taste face. "It's insulting. Like I'm some sort of simple-minded friendly moron who has never had a deep thought in her life." We started to protest (although we were all guilty of underestimating Sunny sometimes) but she held up her hand and continued: "It's not personality, though, it's a way to be that I've chosen for myself. I want to be a psychologist because it seems like . . . it's like professionalized kindness. I think that being kind has power.

"We did all of these interviews and the volume of . . . unkindness was overwhelming. There was one moment though when it was counterbalanced—you were there, Anna, and you too, Ethan—by hearing about one person being a true human." She told the others about the interview with Terrence, how he believed Ethan's brother Gabriel treating him with respect had saved him. We could tell it was important to Sunny by the intensity in her voice when she asked, "Can we talk about the Gabriels in our lives?"

Before we'd even agreed to the idea, Piper started her story—as if it had already been on her mind.

"When I was little my mother always dressed me up in the fanciest clothes on purpose for everyone to say how pretty I was. If they didn't volunteer it by themselves she'd *ask* them, 'Isn't she the prettiest little thing you've ever seen?' My father was the same, always only ever calling me his 'pretty little girl.' Maybe you think that was fun for me but it wasn't. For a long time, that was the only word of praise I knew. It got so I was afraid *not* to be pretty. When I got a bugbite on my face, before my mother taught me to cover it with makeup, I hid in my room terrified for anyone to see me not-pretty.

"Back then my mother was constantly hiring new cleaning ladies who she'd keep for a few months and then trade in for a different model. Appearance was always everything to her and as soon as she heard about someone who did a good job, she'd be convinced they were better than what she had. When I was about four or five my mother hired my Gabriel, who was the only cleaning lady who ever actually talked to me.

"The first day my Gabriel cleaned the kitchen, I brought her my glass when I was done drinking juice instead of leaving it on the table like I guess she expected me to do. My Gabriel said, 'What a thoughtful little girl you are!' I didn't know what 'thoughtful' meant. I asked her if that was another word for 'pretty.' My Gabriel said, 'Oh no! Thoughtful is much more important!' and explained what it meant. After that whenever my Gabriel cleaned the kitchen I would sit in a corner and we would have conversations. Like I was a real person. My Gabriel asked me questions and she *wanted* to know my answers. When I got something right she would tell me how smart I was. If I did something like draw a picture for her she would thank me as if she was genuinely pleased. And if I tried at all to help clean she would show me how to do something simple and tell me, 'Good job!'

"The day came, of course, when my mother told this cleaning lady, like all the others, that she was being replaced. At the end of that day my Gabriel came and found me. She shook my hand and told me solemnly, 'I am very glad to have met you.' I told her I loved her. She didn't hug me—I don't think the cleaning ladies were allowed to hug kids—but she got a big smile on her face that made me feel proud."

"Did you ever see her again?" Hoke asked her. When she shook her head he offered, "When this is all over, if you want I'll help you track her down."

"What would I say to her?"

"Thank you," Sunny offered.

"I'd love that!" Piper beamed.

"Why don't I order that pizza?" Tia suggested before anyone could start on the next Gabriel.

As soon as the order was placed Ethan asked, "My turn? Because I definitely want to clarify: Gabe was not *my* Gabriel." Ethan barely waited for us to laugh before he continued, "I'm proud to have learned that my brother treated someone with a speech impediment kindly but he's still . . . irritating. Therefore, here is my condition: you must all promise never to tell him how we are using his name."

"Who *was* your Gabriel?" Sunny wanted to know, looking delighted with how this conversation was going.

"My father." Ethan sounded wistful. "There are many reasons but this one says it all. Before my father died, we lived in a house. It had a backyard and once when he came home from work my father found me out there crying over a bird that had been mauled to death by a predator. My dad, he sat down and cried with me. He explained that it was important to feel sadness no matter if it hurt. 'But,' he told me, 'never let sadness be an excuse.' When I asked him what that meant he explained that most always there was a lesson in sadness, that if I looked hard enough I could find something I could do to make the future better. Then we searched the shed for enough wood to put together a makeshift birdhouse. We hung it on a tree in order for the *next* bird to have what my father called a 'safety nest.' (Did I mention he was addicted to word plays?) I loved it so much that on my birthday he bought me a bigger, fancier birdhouse. But I always treasured the one we made together best."

Ethan looked around for who was going to talk about their Gabriel next. Jade looked like she did and didn't want to speak. Her sharp angles were sticking out in all directions. She started, "My Gabriel is gone too. She's not dead but . . . I wish . . ." She inhaled brokenly and began again: "When my father was alive my mother was . . . jolly. She giggled a lot and she cooked up wonderful-smelling things and she hugged me whenever I was in touching distance. Then after we lost my father—" Jade's face crumbled. "I can't do this," she whispered.

"Then you don't have to," Tia said quickly. "Anna, do you have a Gabriel you want to tell us about?"

"My Gabriel is gone too," I repeated the way Jade had started like I was just picking up where Ethan left off. "She was the woman who started the Greene Street Shelter. Well, and my first dog there, she was part of the same Gabriel. I have to tell the whole story to explain."

I hadn't been ready to speak so I took a moment to reorganize what I wanted to say.

"I had no one back then. My Gabriel was already dying when I met her. She told me that first thing. 'The pain would not have stopped me,' she explained, 'but the disease, it has finally used me up.' I don't know if she talked to everyone that way but to me, she told only the truth. She wanted me to know why she couldn't bring me along slowly. She wouldn't have time. 'I have this pit bull for you, Anna, but you need to understand they are not like other dogs, not like any other creature I've known. They need love to live like it's as physical for them as food and water. Without it, they shrivel away. With love, they can sometimes survive when science says they can't.' Then she carefully added,

'Sometimes they don't make it though. You need to know that too.' She told me to come back the next day. My pit bull was being ambulanced there that night.

"I rushed straight from school but I was too late. The shelter director had died. The pit was there, a sad mound inside a big crate. She was hooked up to IVs and so drugged out I didn't think she knew when I crawled into her crate with her. When I sat right up against her she took one extra ragged breath but I couldn't tell if that meant anything. I sat with her like that for hours. Every once in a while I tried to pat the few uninjured spots I could find on her head or body. I came back the next day and then every afternoon for a long time. I started bringing my homework and after a while it was simply where I was, where I was supposed to be. I couldn't see any improvement but I didn't think, or I didn't want to think, that she was worse.

"One afternoon I thought I felt a little extra pressure from her against my leg but I convinced myself I hadn't. After a few more days I let myself be sure she was leaning against me. It took a long time. The day she actually put her head in my lap was the happiest I'd ever been. Literally, I could feel my heart warm. From the look in her eyes, I think hers did too. Do you understand? If it hadn't been for my Gabriel—both of them—I wouldn't have known ..."

I stopped talking then but all my friends clamored, "What happened to her?"

"Well, when she started to move around they eased her off the drugs and she healed quicker than anyone expected. Once her body fought off what had been done to it, it turned out she was a joyful dog. Not only me but everyone at the shelter, she stole all our hearts. My favorite shelter worker adopted her. She's old now, especially for a pit, but she still comes to visit every once in a while." I added proudly, "She *always* puts her head in my lap like she did that first time."

Hoke asked, "Can I say something but not answer any questions?" It was obvious it was difficult for him to tell us what was on his mind.

"Yes," Tia promised for all of us.

"Anna is my Gabriel."

Rae-Rae shouted, "That's better than any love lyrics, like ever!"

I started to cry . . . but the good kind.

"My Gabriel was music," Rae-Rae confided. "Is that OK that it isn't a living thing?"

"There's no rules here," Tia our *parliamentarian* assured her.

"I always had all of these *feelings* that I couldn't share or make anyone understand. Then one day my third-grade teacher—oh my god, *he* was my Gabriel—wanted to know what was wrong but I couldn't tell him. He asked me if there was any song I could sing that would say it for me but I confessed I didn't know any songs. The next day in class he played the whole soundtrack from *Cats the Musical*. It took *hours* because he kept stopping and asking us to name the emotions in the songs. I don't remember most of them now except for the one cat who was really sad because she'd gotten old and the other cats didn't want to play with her anymore. It seemed mega unfair. For a long time after that I would try to match up my feelings to a song from *Cats*. After a while I started looking for other songs when *Cats* didn't contain a particular feeling." Rae-Rae giggled at her teenaged self: "I guess I'm never going to find Etta James' 'Roll With Me Henry' in a musical for kids."

We all agreed Rae-Rae's teacher was her Gabriel. Hoke promised to try to help track down that teacher, too, and Rae-Rae vowed to find exactly the right song for the occasion.

"Is it OK to ask you a question though, Rae-Rae?" Hoke, extra-cautious. She nodded. "Why would you think any other third grader was any better than you were at expressing feelings?"

Rae-Rae opened her mouth and no answer came out. "That," she laughed, referring to her momentary freeze. Apparently logic wasn't enough to change her mind.

Tia asked if Dareen wanted to go next. Dareen chose her words meticulously: "I mean no disrespect. My culture invented feminism. But today Islam is, at terrible times, perverted against its daughters. Some Gabriels face arrest and imprisonment or worse for protecting innocents. The word 'urgent,' they see it as a sacred duty. I have been taught all my life to guard the secrecy and safety of such women. I'm sorry but my Gabriels cannot be named."

Tia and Ethan bowed low that way they had with their arms at their sides. The rest of us tried to imitate the gesture.

My mind started to wander to the guesses I'd had before about Dareen's grandmother. Tia brought us back, probably deliberately, by starting her own narrative.

"You've met my Gabriel, the first day we trained with Ethan. I call him my sensei. When I was young my parents sent me to ballet classes." Tia made a lime-puckered face I'm not sure she was conscious of. "I was tall even then, always taller than any of the other pretend ballerinas. Being small was . . . desired. The shorter, thinner, more delicate, and yes whiter that they were, the better the roles and attention. It made me feel . . . cheated, as if I had lost a fixed fight. I didn't slouch—that would not have been permitted from a ballet student—but I let the meanness inside. One day I was, as usual, sitting in the wings while the delicate girls got to dance. My Gabriel—I didn't know him then—was there observing one of the boys who studied both with him and the ballet teachers. The sensei asked if he could sit next to me. He was completely still but there was something about his presence that comforted me. After a while he turned to me, lifted his hand, and asked, 'May I?' When I nodded he ran two fingers down the back of my neck, relaxing and stretching muscles I hadn't known were clenched. 'Never let anyone make you smaller than you are,' he told me. The next day I began my studies with him."

All of us clapped at Tia's Gabriel. What else could we do?

Sunny went last. "My Gabriel was my cousin," she began, "although I sure didn't know that's what she'd turned out to be when this started. She was my age and we were expected to be good friends, which I resented. Then her mother got sick and my mother volunteered for my cousin to come stay with us for however long it took and that I *really* resented. I didn't want to share my room and my things and my life with this interloper. For once, though my mother didn't seem to care about my feelings," Sunny laughed at herself before resuming.

"On the day my cousin was set to move in my mother gave me a serious lecture about how I was supposed to act. I was still simmering when the girl walked in, put down her suitcase, and looked around. She studied the whole place thoughtfully and then offered up, 'I bet you would like bunk beds in here.' I was shocked. She was right. I had *always* wanted bunk beds but I'd always been told no. My cousin winked at me, took me by the hand, and we went in search of my mother. 'Aunt Lilly,' she began, 'you know how you told me I could have whatever I wanted and I told you I didn't want anything and that made you sad?' My mother nodded. 'Well, I've thought about it. I know you told me not to worry about Sunny sleeping in a cot tonight and tomorrow you would get us twin beds. But could we get bunk beds instead?' And . . . my mother said yes!

"That afternoon my mother took us to the supermarket and told my cousin to pick out anything she'd like to eat. As we walked the aisles my eyes strayed to the always-forbidden candy racks. My cousin noticed, stopped short, and looked longingly at the rows of chocolates until my mother finally followed her gaze. My mother told her to choose whatever she wanted! My cousin chose a bag of Snickers—yes, that's where my Snickers obsession comes from—and later shared the bag with me. Really she gave me most of them.

"By then I realized something was up. When we were back in my room alone I got her to explain: 'Aunt Lilly keeps telling me I can have whatever I want, just ask. Every time she says it, it *scares* me, because that must mean Mama is really sick. Aunt Lilly doesn't like it if I say 'nothing,' but that's what it makes me feel like, that I don't want anything except for Mama to get better. When I got here and you looked sad too, I figured it out. *You* want things and if I say I want them, it makes Aunt Lilly happy and I can get them for you which makes *you* happy, and that makes *me* happy.'

"It was such a perfect scam we kept it up until we went too far. The day my Gabriel told my mother she wanted a horse my mother figured it out. By then my aunt was almost recovered though so it would have ended anyway."

"Sunny, that was exactly what we needed!" Rae-Rae told her.

While I was listening, I'd been puzzling over what Sunny had said at the beginning. Now I put the pieces together: "Sunny for me it's more than kindness. I think it's also doing something. And the reverse is that bullying is more than cruelty, it is doing something too. I'm sorry, I don't know how to say this so it makes sense."

"No," Ethan contradicted, "you're brilliant, Anna. That's precisely correct. Sunny is right that kindness has power. Bullying is the antithesis, it's cruelty fueled by power abuse. It creates a negative gestalt. Remember our first conversation when I dismissed as unimportant the students who followed Beemer's lead in sneering at me? I was wrong. It's like Beemer had this negative energy and they accelerated its force. And the students who said nothing because they feared Beemer, they created a vacuum that gave his cruelty more energy. What Gabe did, I'm proud of it. But at most, he was a neutralizer. OBaaT, it is a counter-force. Sorry, I think I mixed scientific metaphors." Hoke nodded.

Tia had been consulting her notes. "Sunny said it, the very first OBaaT meeting: 'It feels like if we ignore it, we're part of what's wrong.' "

"And you said it in our first OBaaT poem," I told Tia:

> Red danger,
> black terror,

yellow caution,
blue sadness ...
*what are the colors of kindness and
courage?*

"We are," we said together.

31

A new secretary or intern or whoever he was ushered Piper and me into the conference room, informing us that "Ms. Horne was detained in court but she will be with you shortly. In the meantime please make yourselves comfortable and help yourselves to our full assortment of beverages." I think the formality was intended to make us feel important but all it did was make us uncomfortable. Piper was probably thinking it felt like we were underdressed at a fancy restaurant. Until the guy said, "Ms. Horne insisted that I order you sandwiches. I'll wait while you select from these menus."

After he left Piper whispered, "I had a mental picture of Naomi megaphoning her warmth into his ear—"

"—and it coming out his mouth pressed flat like a shirt!" I finished, giggling.

"And what's with his eyes? They look like he's allergic to us." Piper, still whispering.

"Maybe he just started wearing contacts." I didn't want to be mean although I knew Piper was being observant, not critical.

Scanning the room, Piper approved in a louder voice, "I like the way this looks. Modern, kind of."

"Me too. It's not all heavy dark wood like her old offices used to be when Ms. Horne worked for a firm. And it's not all plastic and battered like the conference rooms in the courthouse."

"Have you ever been in jail?" Piper slapped her hands over her mouth as if she could stuff the question back in.

"I saw one once," I told her so she would stop feeling bad about asking. "There's always a shortage of beds—places to put foster kids when they come into the system or change placements. A bunch of us had been sleeping on the floor in the Family Services offices. After a couple of days, somebody decided the jail would be a better place to put us. 'At least there will be cots to sleep on,' they told us. When we got to the jail some of the kids started to cry just looking at how scary it was. When he heard them, the night warden or whoever he was came out front. He yelled at Family Services, 'NO! No way. I'm not going to get blamed for this when it gets out. And there *will* be blame.' They brought us back to Family Services and we spent another night on the floor. But word got out anyway—"

"—It's better now," my lawyer assured a now shocked-looking Piper. We hadn't heard her come in. "Better but not good," she continued. "When Family Services tried to pull that stunt at the jail we sued. That's when they came up with the money for teen shelters and a campaign to recruit more foster parents. Occasionally though there are still bed shortages. It's a disgrace." My lawyer stopped herself, apologized, "I didn't mean to eavesdrop."

"I know I can close the door if I want privacy." It felt good that this time it was me assuring her. "That's one of the first things you taught me." I smiled.

"What got you started on the topic of jails?"

I shrugged. *Not mine to tell.* Piper confessed, "I asked."

My lawyer gave Piper a long, assessing look. "After we're done I am available if you want a consultation, Piper."

"And I don't have to be here unless you want me to." I had to say that although it was acknowledging something Piper had kept unspoken.

"First things first," my lawyer suggested. Piper looked like she'd been given a reprieve.

Before we'd left OBaaT, Hoke had handed me one of those USBs with the pdf of our notebook. I passed it to my lawyer who asked permission to give it to her law student intern. We must have made faces because she laughed, "I know. He's acting a little stiff right now. OK stiff as—"

"—an ironed shirt!" Piper and I giggled in unison.

"But"—she gave us her 'this is important' look—"no matter how much he's overreacting to my lecture about restraint, he genuinely hates the mistreatment of children and he's willing to work hard. I think there's hope for him."

It made me proud to be consulted. Piper nodded at me and I agreed for the both of us it was OK for the law student intern to be brought into it.

"Mac," my lawyer told him when he reported to us in the conference room, "my clients have conducted an investigation which is all on this thumb drive. This is time sensitive. I'd like you to back it up and print it out. Then review it, summarize it, and make notes of questions and suggestions that occur to you while I consult with Anna and Piper. Report back here when you're done, all right?"

Mac took the thumb drive, nodded his assent, and literally backed out of the conference room. I was almost disappointed he hadn't bowed. Piper and I exchanged one last eye-roll before getting down to our serious business.

It took a long time to summarize all we had learned and to update Ms. Horne on the confrontation with Berry and the note Ms. Harbinger had passed me.

"OBaaT's activities have clearly become public knowledge. That means it is decision time—" my lawyer started to tell us before Mac appeared at the door.

Somehow he looked more . . . purposeful. Mac handed my lawyer the thumb drive and a large stack of papers with notes all over them. Then he said, dead serious: "He. Must. Be. Stopped." All three of us gestured for him to take a seat.

"Because of Willy?" His seizure still weighed on my conscience.

"Or Terrence?" Tears had formed in Piper's eyes when Ms. Horne had explained the term "elective mutism," that it meant Terrence had stopped talking because it was too painful for him to speak.

Ms. Horne told her that sometimes that happened to child witnesses when they were "questioned" too often before trial. "Especially by amateurs," she added. Anyone can volunteer—"

"—All of them," Mac cut in before Ms. Horne started in on him again about children needing real lawyers. "Maybe especially the child gaslighted into calling himself Squeaky. But most of all, because of Beemer himself."

Mac apologized to my lawyer for "taking such copious notes." I guess Ms. Horne had been working on his ability to get to the point because he did right away: "The one fundamental question I have is how many of the students OBaaT interviewed will be willing to testify."

"We didn't ask," I admitted uncertainly.

"And you were right not to," my lawyer was quick to reassure me. "It's wrong to draft 'volunteers' without declaring war." I didn't really understand how volunteers could be drafted until later in the conversation.

"Here's where I think we should start our strategizing," Ms. Horne offered, taking me completely by surprise by the challenge: "Define success."

My brain spun in a million different impossible-outcome directions. *Rein it in.* "I know what failure feels like. The only thing that happened to Beemer for causing Willy's seizure was he disappeared for a week. I heard he even got full pay for the time off. If anything, Beemer was worse after that."

Piper was more direct. "It would make me really happy if I never had to see his face again." She corrected herself as if she needed to clarify: "*Beemer's* face."

"I get that. But here's something to consider." My lawyer filled us in on the bad news: "There is a horrible practice called 'pass the trash.' It refers to when a teacher or really any education professional is finally caught out and instead of being disciplined, he or she is allowed to resign and is re-employed someplace else."

"Wouldn't they need like references or something?" Piper asked.

"Do you think The Tsar would voluntarily tell anyone what he allowed to go on at his school?" My lawyer's logic was depressing.

"Does that mean that we have to take down The Tsar?" I asked but then I had to giggle at sounding like a Russian revolutionary.

Piper and my lawyer smiled with me. Mac observed with what looked like straight-faced determination, "No firing squad necessary." I was definitely going to have to learn how to read him.

"I think what Mac means is that, if we decide that's our goal, we have a chance—and remember that's all it is—of having what you uncovered about Beemer public enough that it would be against The Tsar's self-interest to support him."

"Can we do that?" Me.

"How can we do that?" Piper.

My lawyer did not look happy when Mac answered, "It depends on what price you are willing to pay."

"No," my lawyer corrected him, "OBaaT has nothing to prove about courage and determination. I am very proud of what you have already accomplished no matter where we take it from here." Softening, she continued, "I can lay out your choices but I want you to understand I'm not advocating for any one of them over the others." She gave Mac a hard look. He rearranged the paperwork in front of him.

"Tell us," we asked her, feeling a little bad for Mac but taller in our seats for how she was speaking to us.

"One choice would be to leak the information in your notebook to the press. We'd have to find the right reporter and these days that's harder than it used to be because there's a lot less investigative reporting. We would redact—block out—the names of witnesses and victims which means it would be a dice roll how seriously the public would take it. Typically, Beemer would minimize the accusations and complain about over-entitled students and parents who litigate every much-deserved bad grade. And The Tsar would wave the flag about how we all should be grateful to be back in a real school. Still, because it would bring them unwanted attention, it has the possibility of improving their conduct."

"But not much of a possibility?" Piper questioned.

"Unpredictable." The word came out of Mac's mouth without him expecting it to. He resumed his absorption with his papers.

"Yes," Ms. Horne conceded, "it's not the kind of story that would definitely capture and keep public attention but it has that potential with the local press. It is about the only option I can think of that does not require OBaaT to participate. I have to say, though, that going public is extremely iffy. I usually reserve it for when all else fails."

"Might as well tweet," Mac snorted to himself.

From the way my lawyer paused, she would definitely be having a *long* talk with Mac after we'd left. In front of us she said, "Perhaps I should explain why I don't think internet outreach is viable as an option."

"We know," I assured her, flashing on Hoke calling his "#BeamOnBeemer" idea stupid.

"I thought about it," Piper admitted, making me regret having spoken first, "like why couldn't there be a #MeToo for bullying? Anna's Hoke found one for us where victims can post their experiences. But I don't think it would work for OBaaT and I don't think I'd want it to."

"Why not?" Ms. Horne encouraged.

"At the beginning, it was exciting to watch women . . . change the world, really. But now I guess it's like the world has a short attention span. The times I see #MeToo making a difference, it's because people have organized to make change in the real world. Does that make sense?"

"It's genius, Piper," I assured her. "The first idea I had was to start an OBaaT Facebook page; like that would somehow make it real. But Facebook, it's like everyone wants to post their own opinion, and that's *all* they want. No listening. No doing anything." My lawyer smiled wryly which gave me the courage to continue: "We talked a lot about this, Ms. Horne." I tried to repeat Ethan's words: "That the essence of bullying is that it gives power to cruelty. We want to be a counterbalance. We're not going to do that on the internet. And from what it sounds like, we can't expect to do that in the local news either."

This time Mac muttered "Brava!" under his breath.

"You said the press was 'one choice,' " I prompted my lawyer.

"At the opposite end of the extreme from going public is suing."

Mac sat up straight making it obvious we had reached *his* choice. This guy should never try to keep secrets.

"Who could we sue?" Piper asked.

"You get right to the point," my lawyer approved. "In theory, at least the students who have been directly harmed by Beemer could sue him. To sue anyone else, those defendants would have to have known about Beemer's conduct and failed to act."

"The Tsar will be off the hook unless we complain to him first?" I hated that idea.

"That's probably an over-simplification of the law and I don't mean to make it sound like you all personally would have to bring these facts to the principal's attention. But, for practical purposes, yes."

"I don't understand," Piper and I told her at the same time.

"OK, the most overtly injured people you've uncovered are Terrence, Willy, and Squeaky. Terrence was mute and Willy had a seizure. Maybe we could argue that the school should have known and investigated why those events happened. We don't have even that much with Squeaky."

"And except for Terrence, we don't know if they'd be willing to testify," I added. *That's what she meant by drafting volunteers!*

"We would need willing plaintiffs," she confirmed.

"And those are our only choices?" Even to me my question sounded defeated.

"Oh, definitely not. I'm sorry if I've discouraged you. I want you to look at *all* your choices because you have big decisions to make. Maybe I shouldn't have started with the least likely ones."

I pulled out the half-forgotten slip of paper Mrs. Harbinger had given me: 'Colton Bridgeway; Adams County District School Board Member; cell phone.' "This is our best choice?"

"That's exactly what I've been trying to find out," my lawyer admitted. "I don't practice what's called 'school law' but I've been checking around. If you did want to sue, I think I've found a group of lawyers for children who would take the case. But they'd probably file complaints with various agencies first anyway. I don't know much background information about most of those agencies and it's hard to tell how sincere they are. The only other person I know in the field is the lawyer for the school board. He's a decent sort but the school board is his client which means we need to take his opinion with a grain of salt."

"What opinion?" Mac asked, forgetting again what his role was supposed to be.

"The school board will take complaints—actually we could send your report directly to the lawyer I talked to. But he admitted that you'd get taken more seriously if the issue was raised by a school board member. He thinks Bridgeway is our best bet."

"Did he say why?" I questioned, wondering how much I could trust my creative writing teacher.

"He was vague but I did my own research. School board members are elected. The ones who've held the position here a long time are traditional and conservative. This recent election though, some reform candidates ran. Several of them had the energy to win seats no one expected. Of that group, Bridgeway is the most credible. He's young. But levelheaded."

"So we should call him?"

"There's one more decision you would need to make." I sighed. I love how respectful my lawyer is but sometimes I wish she'd just tell me what to do. "Would you like me to call him for you or would you rather do that yourselves?"

"Would he take it more seriously if *you* called?" Piper asked Ms. Horne.

"He might. But in my book that would be a strike against him. If he were responsive to a call from a student, that would give us much more information about his sincerity, whether we could trust him."

"I'll call," I said, not sure if I was convinced or simply needed to stop debating what to do. OBaaT had left this decision in my hands.

. . .

"Speakerphone or privacy?" Ms. Horne again.

"I'd like your help if I get lost."

Mac set up the speakerphone so we could all hear and I dialed, not really expecting an answer.

"Bridgeway here."

I gave him my name. "I . . . I'm a student at"—*I almost said 'The Boring Brick Building'!*—"of Frederick Beemer. He's a teacher at Adams High School—"

"Yes Anna, I'm familiar with his name from reports."

It kind of sounded like Mr. Bridgeway was trying to make it easier on me. I closed my eyes so I could concentrate, took a big gulp of air, and then tried to say it all at once: "My friends and I, we were upset about how he was treating some of his students. We did an investigation and prepared a report. We'd like to give it to you."

"I'd be very interested to see it."

"The thing is, could we give it to you without the names of everyone we interviewed? If you agree to, well whatever you decide to do about our report, we could go back and get permission but we don't have it now."

"That would be fine, Anna. I admire you respecting their confidentiality. Let me find out what we're dealing with first before we worry about invading anyone's privacy."

I opened my eyes and made my eyebrows into a question. Ms. Horne looked pleased. Piper looked impressed. Mac redeemed himself by sliding over a printout of OBaaT's report with the names already deleted.

"I have it right here!" I told Mr. Bridgeway.

"Excellent."

"Could you hold on a minute?" I asked. I covered the phone with my hand, not sure how to make arrangements. Ms. Horne pointed to herself then made an is-it-OK? gesture with her hands.

"I'm at my lawyer's office. Can she talk to you for a minute?"

"Of course." If Mr. Bridgeway was surprised, it didn't show in his voice.

"Naomi Horne here. I'd rather not send the report electronically"—*That's right! Hoke warned me emailing a pdf was not secure*—"but we can messenger it to you if you'd like. We'll include our contact information. What address should we deliver it to?"

"I'm at my office." He sounded businesslike. He gave us the address and suddenly the conversation was over.

. . .

Piper and I grinned. Ms. Horne suggested we take a break because "I think we need to celebrate." Mac headed off back to his paperwork while we went across the street to a fancy coffee/ice cream shop. Ms. Horne, who told me, "Call me Naomi for this," treated us to shakes and herself to a latte. We clinked coffee-house-labeled cups, toasting, "To OBaaT!"

On the way back Piper whispered, "No questions and no telling *anyone*, promise?" I nodded, ashamed that I'd completely forgotten her consult with my lawyer. Ms. Horne hadn't. She led us back to her private office, asking Piper's permission before shutting the door.

Then, silence. Looking at Piper I flashed on Terrence losing his voice because it was too hard to talk. *What bully did this to my friend?*

Ms. Horne asked gently, "What made you ask about jail, Piper?"

Piper's question for my lawyer tumbled out of her: "Can someone get a restraining order if they haven't been hit?"

Ms. Horne went into explain-the-law mode: "Well, Piper there's all sorts of protective orders. Usually, when you hear about restraining orders, it's a domestic violence case—between family members, or people who live together, or people in a sexual relationship. And yes, they usually involve battering. There are other kinds of protective orders to help in other situations. I should add that no matter what kind, you are right that the consequences of violating a protective order could well be jail . . . but that tends to happen only when that is the only way to enforce them."

Piper wanted specifics: "What other kinds of protective orders are there?"

I thought Ms. Horne's answer had unsaid questions underneath each phrase. She started again with the least likely: "Protective orders can be against elder abuse; against abuse of someone with a physical or mental disability; to protect someone who has been sexually assaulted . . ." She paused longer after that one but we saw no response. "And there are anti-stalking orders." *That one.* Ms. Horne saw it too.

"Stalking, that's like when someone won't leave you alone?" Piper, small-voiced.

"Yes." No one was more patient than my lawyer when she chose to be.

Finally, into this second silence, Piper confided, "It's my boyfriend Lance. I keep trying to break up with him but he won't let me."

I bit my lip to stay quiet. Thankfully Ms. Horne asked it: "What does he do?"

"Sometimes he ignores me when I try to tell him this isn't working. Like I haven't said anything at all. Other times, he yells at me and calls me awful names. Either way, it frightens me. A lot."

"What are you frightened *of*?"

"It's not that Lance threatens me. But it feels . . . out of control."

"There are all sorts of threats, Piper," my lawyer said carefully. "For example, someone who punches a wall can make you feel it's really you that they want to punch. Or someone who takes personal pictures of you without your knowledge, there's a threat there that they might share them or post them online without your consent. Or someone who says they'll kill themselves if you leave—that's putting death on the table."

Everything about Piper except her mouth said that she'd been threatened all those ways. She shuddered but stayed quiet. This time waiting her out didn't work.

"I tell you what, Piper," Ms. Horne finally suggested, "why don't you start a notebook like the one you've worked on for OBaaT? Whenever Lance frightens you, write down the date, time, and place, who was there, and what specifically was said and done. That way you'll have a record and, if you decide to, you can bring it to me and we can apply for a stalking order. No guarantees. Some judges are better than others about granting them. But with a record like that, we'll have a good chance."

Piper nodded which I thought meant that she agreed to a Lance notebook, but then she added, "I think I want to try one last time to make him understand it's over."

"Lots of stalking victims feel like that. And I can understand it. Do me one favor though? Don't have that conversation alone. Make sure to have a witness. Someone you trust. Preferably someone who can protect you physically."

Until that last sentence, Piper had begun to look relieved. Now she was back to looking frightened. "I can ask my father," she faltered.

"Good deal," my lawyer concluded.

Almost before those words were out of Ms. Horne's mouth, Piper turned to me: "Anna, I can't wait to tell everyone we sent OBaaT's report to the school board. Naomi, thank you for everything." *Not subtle Piper.*

I tried to add my thanks to Piper's but my lawyer wouldn't listen to us. She did agree to pass along our appreciation to Mac. *Along with a few choice words I bet.* "It was so cool he had already deleted the names from OBaaT's report for Mr. Bridgeway."

"Anna, if you ever decide to go to law school, you come to me for a job."

There are words I keep in my heart forever.

32

Almost before I'd gotten back to the Good Farmers', my lawyer texted me that Colton Bridgeway wanted a few days, "to give this report the attention it deserves," and that he would probably want to meet with us next week. I group-texted OBaaT an update, thinking how hard waiting was going to be. When my phone pinged right away I expected commiseration, but it was Charity instead. Would everyone from OBaaT come to the teen shelter to see her Saturday afternoon at 1:00? The shelter had never given her those day passes we'd hoped for—maybe being a runaway had prevented that—but they'd let Rae-Rae and I visit once a week. This would be the first time Charity met the rest of us.

Last week we'd held a solemn private ceremony, just the three of us. Charity's mother had been hospitalized again. "In a strange way, I didn't feel as helpless this time," Charity confessed. "I guess because I wasn't there, living it with her. Don't hate me for being selfish but I was almost glad, knowing they can't send me back to her now."

Rae-Rae tapped her phone to play "Sometimes I Feel like a Motherless Child," a version by someone I'd never heard of named Helen Merrill. Rae-Rae said she was a famous jazz singer but what was important was this version was more accepting than sad.

Maybe Rae-Rae's song meant the same thing as I did when I gave Charity a yo-yo. I'd painted a circle on each side with a slash through it. "No more yo-yoing."

Charity's text didn't say why she wanted all of us there this Saturday but later Rae-Rae spilled the beans enough that we all knew to bring presents. It was an easy pick: art supplies.

Mrs. Meeny, the teen shelter director, wasn't around when I got there but she'd arranged paper plates and napkins on a waiting-for-cake table. Nothing could make the shelter look merry, but the air was somehow softer than usual. And when Charity rushed in to greet me, she looked . . . lit from inside. I had a split second of sadness when I realized I'd never seen her happy before. But regret didn't have a chance on that day, in that room.

When Rae-Rae had said "celebration" I'd thought she knew more than she was telling us. But she was as surprised as anyone at Charity's bursting-with-news excitement. Charity was so delighted keeping us in suspense that we didn't press her.

I recognized a few of the residents although they were shy in the background once Ethan and Sunny, Rae-Rae, Tia and Dareen, Hoke, and even Jade and Piper crowded the room with party spirits. Mrs. Meeny poked her head in, waited for a nod from Charity, and then wheeled in a huge sheet cake. It was frosted in plain white with only four little scattered sections that had red writing on them. Each saying had an exclamation point after it.

"Congrats!" "Bon Voyage!" "Proud of You!" "We'll Miss You!" Mrs. Meeny pulled out a bag of those colored-icing squeeze bottles.

"Charity has an announcement for all of you. She wants to tell you her news first, and then you can use these"—she held up the squeeze bottles—"to write messages to her. When you're all done, I'll take a photo for Charity to keep. Then we can cut the cake!"

More residents slid into the corners of the room. I didn't think it was the cake that drew them, but the hope in the air. That's rare and precious in our world.

"OK, OK. I can't stand waiting another minute," Charity laughed. "I am the luckiest person ever. Mrs. Meeny, I don't know how to thank you." Charity stifled an unexpected sob in her throat and had to take a minute before she could continue. "All of us—" She looked at me and some of the residents behind us. "On our brave days we have dreams. Mine are coming true."

Charity explained that she'd completed her GED at the teen shelter and tomorrow (*Wow!*) she was getting on a bus for Chicago. She'd been selected for admission to the Promising Young Artists program. She'd be taking remedial courses until next fall when she would start . . . college! "Like a real freshman!" she said. A scholarship and transition-from-foster-care money would help pay her expenses, but she also had a job waiting in the university bookstore. And a real dorm room. She turned to Mrs. Meeny: "No offense!

"Speech! Speech!" Charity started the shout to Mrs. Meeny and we all joined in.

"When I think about why I do this work"—Mrs. Meeny looked serious—"I remember the moments when I was able to ease someone's sadness or right a wrong. You all have reminded me that moments like this are as important." She refused to say any more words. She didn't need to.

While everyone crowded around the cake to write their icing messages, I walked over to stand by Hoke. I wasn't sure how all this would hit him. "If you ever wonder if OBaaT is worth it," he told me, "you think of this moment too."

By the time I walked over to the cake with my squeeze bottle, it looked like a bakery version of the high school yearbook most of us would never own—a jumble of words and signatures and personal doodles, in a bed of frosting. "I'll never forget you!" "Don't ever change!" "You're so lucky!" "Remember me when you're famous!" "You're finally free!" "Proud of you!" "Stay cool!" "I wish I could have known you better!"

I found a tiny space that was still blank and iced my phone number onto the cake. *Don't forget me.* I hate goodbyes.

After the party, how emotional the week had been caught up with me. I decided I needed some pit bull therapy. I took a bus to Greene Street to walk two of my favorites, a large white scary-looking guy and his pretty honey-colored mate-for-life. Despite appearances, he was the tender-hearted goofus and she was the always-one-step-ahead-of-him boss. Her favorite way to torment him was to invent a new game moments before he had mastered the last one. I let them wrestle in a quiet corner of the park. Preventing their leashes from tangling challenged all my dexterity, but their pure joy made it worth it. Once they were semi-exhausted we ambled around. With a mother's permission, I allowed the honey-colored one to lick a willing baby's outstretched hand. The baby laughed at the slobber deposit.

I let the white one munch on grass, a forbidden addiction he tended to indulge in at any stolen opportunity. On the walk back I had to finger comb grass shards out of his muzzle. "You'll never make it as a master criminal," I informed him

33

It was Tuesday afternoon by the time Ms. Horne and I met with Colton Bridgeway. At *his* suggestion, we met in *her* office. "For the privacy," he'd said. A normal-seeming secretary escorted me back. If Mac was around, I didn't see him. Even though I'd been warned, the man sitting opposite my lawyer surprised me by looking a lot younger than I had expected from his voice. Still, he had an open face that was somehow reassuring.

"You don't know me," Mr. Bridgeway started right off. "I don't expect you to trust me until you do." *I like him already.* "I will lay out what I have in mind, you can ask me any questions you want, and if you say 'no,' we'll come up with another plan."

It felt like Mr. Bridgeway was talking to both of us. He waited for each of us to agree before he continued.

"When I first heard about students collecting complaints against a teacher"— *Does* everybody *know already?*—"my expectations were guarded. But this"—he held up the printout of our notebook—"is remarkable work. Very powerful.

"My goal is to find a way to make the Adams County District School Board response worthy of the effort. You probably know that I am new to the board. I ran as a reform candidate, which I'm sure did not win me many friends among the sitting members. They also distrust me because of my age—most of them are at least a generation older and, they believe, wiser. So far at least, they have been cordial but I don't know who or how many of them I can count on. I can promise my own support but no one else's."

"Understood." Ms. Horne's approval sounded tentative. "Would you be willing to tell us why you decided to run?"

The question derailed Mr. Bridgeway for a moment. He began, "I'm a working guy," but then paused. We could almost see him considering and rejecting the slogans he'd used in his campaign. "All my life I've been good with my hands. My friends, my teachers, everyone assumed that meant I was no good with my brain. Maybe my ego wants to prove them wrong. I'm a problem solver. Being on the school board, that's my chance to fix more than electrical systems."

My lawyer slid over a magazine article with Colton Bridgeway's photo on the front. "Isn't that a little humble for someone who's been called 'the future of this city'?"

"My sources were right that you always do your homework, Ms. Horne."

"Cards on the table, Mr. Bridgeway. I am very fond of Anna and all of the young people involved in OBaaT. I also have deep respect for what they are trying to accomplish. I've never been one to object to people doing the right thing for the wrong reasons. If your motivation is political ambition, if you see this effort as a potential stepping stone for you personally, I really don't care . . . so long as your conduct is wholly consistent with their goals."

Mr. Bridgeway gave a low whistle under his breath, I guess at my lawyer's bluntness. He switched gears: "Let me tell you my idea." He had our attention.

"I've been studying what research there is on teacher bullying. Most all of the anti-bullying efforts are aimed at student-on-student interaction. Power abuse by teachers is rarely addressed, and more rarely addressed effectively. A few schools have tried an approach that makes sense to me but it is still experimental. It starts with the premise that schools are uncomfortable and inefficient at fact finding—that's the right term?"

Ms. Horne nodded.

"If school boards want to be effective they have to devise a system that seems fair. Yes?"

This time Ms. Horne and I both nodded.

"This new idea is, if a complaint is filed against a teacher or administrator, then without having to admit any wrongdoing, they have the option of avoiding a hearing altogether." Mr. Bridgeway paused again, waiting for more assurance we were following him.

"How would that work?" Ms. Horne obliged him.

"The bully gets a free pass?" was my question.

"No. That's the beauty of it. He only gets a free pass if he signs a contract agreeing he will not engage in the specific conduct in the future."

"That *is* beautiful," Ms. Horne admired, way ahead of me.

When I looked confused she turned to me: "Say a complaint was filed on Squeaky's behalf. Beemer could argue that he'd never said anything to Squeaky or that if he had, it wasn't bullying. A timid school board would have an excuse not to discipline him. Under this system though, Beemer would be asked to sign a contract that *in the future* he would not call the student 'Squeaky' or comment on his wheelchair or disability in any way and he would concede that any such comments would be bullying. Either Beemer corrects his behavior for the future—and I honestly do not think he's capable of that—or else it would be much easier to prove bullying if he violated the contract. Either way, we win."

"Why would Beemer sign then?" I asked both of them.

"It would look pretty bad for him to refuse," Mr. Bridgeway answered, "but I think you're right: at this point Beemer feels entitled, immune from consequences. My prediction is, he'd say 'no way.' "

"You want us to agree to this experimental process and you want all of OBaaT to be willing to go to a hearing if Beemer declines." The way Ms. Horne said it, it didn't sound much like a question.

"Yes," Mr. Bridgeway and I said at the same time.

"As much as I admire your courage, Anna," my lawyer cautioned me gently, "I think we should find out what a hearing would entail before we decide." She was right of course.

"I asked Joshua Jones—the school board lawyer—exactly that question." Mr. Bridgeway consulted his notes: "He says the board can choose to consider the entire OBaaT report as a complaint. The hearing would be conducted by the school board chairman. Jones would be present to advise. The board could accept the OBaaT report as evidence, but it would also need testimony. The chairman would do the initial questioning but Beemer would have a teacher's union lawyer present who would also be allowed to ask the witnesses questions."

Bridgeway turned to Ms. Horne: "Jones said to tell you there would be 'relaxed evidentiary rules.' "

My lawyer explained to me, "It's not like a trial where lawyers jump up and object. It's more informal but still not like normal conversation. Beemer's lawyer could ask questions and he might try to be confrontational. A lot of these union lawyers, they put on a big show so the union will keep them on retainer. It would be up to the chairman and Joshua Jones—the school board lawyer—to control him." She thought about it for a minute and then added, "I would be there too." When I smiled with relief she clarified, "But I would not have any official role. I could not protect you as I do in a courtroom."

I thought about the long discussion Piper and I had had with Ms. Horne, how this was our best chance. "I want to do this," I volunteered, "but I can only speak for myself."

"Will you speak to the other members of OBaaT?" Mr. Bridgeway inquired.

"Yes. But I would have done that whether or not you asked. We've come this far *together*. They left the decision up to me about the report. But they have a right to know what's going on and what their choices are."

"Anna," Ms. Horne requested, "will you also ask OBaaT's permission for me to turn over the unredacted report—with all the names of the people you interviewed in it—to the school board lawyer? I would only do that if I had his assurances that no one would be forced to testify against their will."

"Oh!" Mr. Bridgeway looked embarrassed. "I was supposed to mention this as well." He read word-for-word from his notes: "'Please inform Anna's lawyer that I will advise the Adams

County District School Board that for purposes of this hearing, they do not'—he made me underline the word 'not'—'have subpoena power over students or former students."

Ms. Horne smiled for the first time in the meeting. "OK, one problem solved, Anna. That means if OBaaT is willing to release the names, it will be up to the people you interviewed whether or not to participate in the hearing."

Mr. Bridgeway asked me if I wanted him or maybe my lawyer to be the one to explain these decisions to my friends. Ms. Horne frowned. Until I drew myself up to answer: "If I didn't understand it enough to explain it, I would not have agreed."

. . .

"How many times do we have to tell you 'yes,' Anna?" Tia was beginning to sound exasperated.

"She wants to make sure we *understand*." Rae-Rae, teasing and serious at the same time, held up her hand in a mock pledge, humming Roy Orbison: "Running Scared."

"That we only agreed to send the names of people we interviewed because no one will be forced to testify—" Ethan smiled as he and everyone else held up a hand and hummed along.

"—And that Naomi trusts the school board lawyer not to pressure anyone either—" Piper continued the pledge.

"—And we each understand it is our own personal decision—" Hoke smiled solemnly at me.

"—If we ourselves choose to testify—" Jade vowed, more serious than the others.

"—And that none of us will judge any of the rest of us who might not want to—" Sunny, of course, was the one who added that reassurance to the pledge.

"—And most important of all—" Dareen started the wrap-up.

"—We all promise ourselves that no matter what happens, with the complaint, or during a hearing, or whatever the board decides—" Tia recited.

"—We will *all* be proud of ourselves," I completed the pledge, throwing my hands up in surrender to the discussion being over.

Rae-Rae finished it by singing the victorious last lines of the song: "My heart was breaking, which one would it be? You turned around and walked away with me."

That satisfied Dareen for about a hot minute and then she sighed, followed by her announcing, "We need to *do* something."

We all groaned. We'd practiced at the dojo—I'd finally learned to call it that—for well over an hour while Hoke was finishing up a training session for his coding competition. Then he'd joined us for this intense conversation. How much more "doing" did Dareen think we had in us?

"I know," Tia volunteered. "Here, I'll show you." She did a complicated series of stretches, bends, and postures that I could not have duplicated if my life depended on it. "It's easy," Tia tried to tell us but we knew better.

Ethan talked us into it, explaining each posture while he had us try it. Tia chimed in demonstrating the breathing that went with each position. *C'mon people!* When we'd done a few rounds of what Ethan called "sun salutation," we stopped falling over or hopping around midway through poses. I would never admit it to Tia, or Dareen, or Ethan, but I started feeling more relaxed until . . . the ping I'd been anticipating sounded on my phone.

"Complaint filed."

"now B decides?"

"No. B already refused to sign a contract. He's on paid administrative leave. Now we have a hearing."

"when?"

"Probably next week. IWLYK." *I don't know anyone besides
my lawyer who used that shorthand for 'I will let you know.'* "One
more thing."

"?"

"Congratulations!"

"thank you you always know what to say"

I held my phone screen up to my friends. Rae-Rae swung me
around, shouted "Danny and the Juniors," and started something that felt like jitterbugging "At the Hop." The rest of my
friends joined the dancing. I don't think anyone before us had
ever considered a school board hearing a "hop," but we were
definitely going to rock and roll.

34

"From what Joshua Jones implied," my lawyer whispered to OBaaT, "originally the school board chairman was only indulging Bridgeway when he agreed the board should ask Beemer to sign a contract. The chairman literally laughed at the idea: 'Who would say no to this?' When Beemer refused and demanded a teachers' union lawyer, the chairman was furious—as if he'd been made a fool of. That's when the chairman ordered OBaaT's complaint filed and the hearing scheduled."

We were all in a back room in the Adams County School District office building waiting for the school board's "closed session" meeting to be over. Theoretically, this back room was private but Ms. Horne still kept her voice down so only we could hear.

As excited as we were that this day had come, we were nervous.

The school board's lawyer had led us to this room, introducing himself as Joshua Jones, and explained briefly what we should expect: Beemer's hearing would be open to the public. The full school board would hear evidence. Once the public school board meeting began, we would all be allowed to sit in.

Be prepared that Beemer and his lawyer would be present as well. The board had scheduled two-hour sessions each weekday evening until testimony was complete. At this point he could not predict which of us might testify or on which night.

Mr. Jones had smiled briefly at my lawyer and left us alone.

Tia informed Ms. Horne that I had prepared them all to testify. She said it loudly as if she hoped someone was listening in.

"Yes," Dareen explained at full volume too, "Anna told us what you always say to witnesses."

"Always tell the truth." Jade.

"Be yourself." Sunny.

"Ask if you don't understand a question." Ethan.

"Never guess." Piper. "It's OK to say 'I don't know' or 'I don't remember.' "

"Don't argue with the attorney for the other side." Rae-Rae.

"And don't volunteer. Answer those questions 'yes' or 'no' if you can." Hoke.

By the time they were all done, Ms. Horne looked amused despite herself. "I guess I do say all of that a lot, don't I?"

. . .

There was a lot of bustling and rustling as we all filed into the board hearing chambers. Our lawyer edged us gently away from the Beemer side of the room. At the front was an elevated platform where the board members sat in comfortable padded desk chairs behind a conference table. In front of each one was a placard with their name and title on it. Dead center in that row was a larger-than-the-rest padded chair with a microphone set up in front of it where the portly man I guessed was the chairman sat. Yes, that's what his placard read. The school board lawyer, Joshua Jones, sat in a regular chair slightly behind the chairman. Colton Bridgeway, the school board member who'd helped us file the complaint, was the only other familiar face at the conference table. He was seated in a stuffed chair at the end of the row on the side closest to us. My lawyer whispered to us that the closer board members sat to the chairman, the longer they'd held the title.

Along each side of the meeting room there were smaller tables. One seemed to hold employees of the board with signs in front of them like "Recorder" and "Staff Assistant." The other table was now starting to fill up. It had signs that read "Reserved" and "Press." A guard walked over and shook his head no to a woman who had started to unpack a camera.

In between the wooden benches crowding most of the room and the raised platform for the board, there were two microphoned tables set up to face the school board. Beemer was seated at one of them with his head bent over some papers. He looked greasy. There was a pinch-faced guy next to him—whispering in his ear—who must be the teachers' union lawyer. The table to the right of them was empty. I figured that's where the witnesses would sit. As the wooden benches quickly filled, the air turned somber.

The chairman tapped his microphone in a sound check, led us in a pledge of allegiance, and then called the board meeting to order with words that sounded like he'd repeated them a lot of times before. Just when I had drawn in a breath and thought, *This is it!* the chairman started reading off announcements and conducting what he called "routine board business." *A whole stupid agenda!* At one point Rae-Rae's breathing sounded like

she was about to get the nervous giggles but then she muttered
a quiet "ow" that I figured meant Tia had elbowed her out of it.
I realized I was holding on to Sunny's hand too tightly and tried
to will myself into calm

35

The chairman's drone was so monotonous I almost missed it when he announced that the board would "forthwith turn its attention to a serious matter that has come before it." The now-crowded room seemed to have a quickened pulse. I sure did.

The school board lawyer handed the chairman a piece of paper and he read off of it as if it were his own words. Most of it was officialese that didn't seem to matter until it got to the part about how the hearing would be conducted. The chairman and Beemer would be allowed to make statements, then witnesses would be called, probably over the course of several sessions. *I know this part already.* The witnesses would give what the chairman called "narratives" and the chairman and board members could ask clarifying questions and Beemer's attorney would be permitted to ask questions too. The hearing would begin with "direct evidence" but after that "hearsay witnesses" would also be allowed. He explained, "In order to protect the confidentiality of students who wish to remain anonymous, other students will be permitted to testify to their hearsay statements." He nodded toward the row we were seated in and then continued. Beemer could call his own witnesses if he wanted. The board would then retire to deliberate. Their decision would be announced within two weeks of the conclusion of the hearing. *Please just get to it.* "Are there any procedural questions? No? Then we will begin."

Instead of an opening statement, the chairman read off what was mostly a summary of OBaaT's report which he called "the complaint." The audience murmured. They sounded angry to me but maybe that was only because I wanted them to be.

Beemer's pinch-faced lawyer stood self-importantly, pivoted abruptly to face both the board and the press, and accused: "Today is a disgraceful day in the history of the Adams County School District. A fine teacher with years of exemplary service to the students he diligently instructs has been vilified by unfounded, baseless accusations from a gang of bored overprivileged and disgruntled underprivileged teenagers. At the end of this hearing, I fully expect my client's entire exoneration. I only hope the Adams County District School Board will have the decency to afford him in writing the apology he so thoroughly deserves for being subjected to this indignity."

"Mistake," Ms. Horne muttered under her breath. I tried to figure out why. Oh. He'd just insulted the board that was going to judge his client.

The first witness was a worn-down-looking woman in her forties who was wearing some kind of scrubs. She apologized for the way she was dressed, explaining that she was a nurse who had come directly from work. She was here to talk about her son: "My boy has juvenile diabetes. From the time he was first diagnosed all he ever wanted was to live a normal life. The first day he was finally mainstreamed he was excited. It did my heart good to see him that happy. When he came home from school that day—" She interrupted herself, pointed at Beemer, spit out, "You, you're a monster."

"I know this is upsetting but we would ask that you refrain from name-calling during your testimony," the chairman admonished her.

"I'm sorry, judge," she apologized. The chairman liked the title too much to correct her. For a fraction of a moment when she turned her face away from him, I thought I saw a hint of a smile but I must have been mistaken.

The nurse needed a pause before she could continue. "My son left for school full of hopes and expectations. When he came home that day he was a different, broken boy. He has never been the same since."

"Different in what way?" our ally Colton Bridgeway asked gently when the narrative seemed to have stalled again.

"He was bent over crying and he told me he was never going back to school. When I went to put my arm around him I realized he smelled bad, he had wet himself. Urinary urgency— needing to pee badly enough that it is difficult to control—is a symptom of juvenile diabetes. My son hadn't had that problem for years but I thought it might have been the stress of his big day. It took him a long time to tell me the truth. He only admitted it because I checked one too many times whether he was having trouble with his kidneys."

"What did he tell you?" This time it was the chairman who asked.

"My son was doing fine in all his first-day classes. Then in Mr. Beemer's class, he felt the need to urinate. He asked permission to leave but Mr. Beemer refused. The more my son's body needed relief, the more cruel Beemer became. Beemer told him, 'If you can't hold it, you don't belong in a real school,' 'What does the baby want *this* time?' and 'Maybe you need someone to hold it for you for you to do the job right.' Finally, my son realized he had to leave whether he had permission or not, but when he got up, just the motion, that's when he had the accident. Beemer pointed at him, snorted out scorn, and got his students to jeer as well."

By now the woman's voice and posture had stiffened with anger. The crowd was with her. Beemer's lawyer demanded loudly, "Move to strike, hearsay."

The school board lawyer whispered in the chairman's ear and the chairman repeated out loud, "Hearsay is permitted in this hearing." Mr. Jones whispered again, longer this time. The chairman announced for the record, "Also, there are no motions to strike. This is not a criminal trial. The rules of evidence are relaxed."

Ms. Horne side-mouthed to me, "He should say 'no questions.' " But Beemer's lawyer didn't agree.

"Isn't it a fact, madam, that your son is an invalid who should never have been permitted to attend school among *normal* children?"

"What are you saying?" the witness tried to protest, sitting up even straighter. The chairman cut her off, yelling at the lawyer, "That's not the law."

Quick consult between Beemer and his lawyer. "Do you know for a fact that Frederick Beemer was aware of your son's medical condition?"

"His diabetes was in all of his school records and the school nurse assured me—health professional to health professional—

that she would speak to each of his teachers and explain my son's special needs."

"So you admit your son has 'special needs.' " He put an ugly emphasis on the phrase.

"Thank you," she answered incongruously. The witness's voice had weapons in it, but she was almost drowned out.

"That's enough, sir," the chairman bellowed. "There will be no more questions along those lines to any witness in this hearing, do you understand?"

"If you are not going to let me do my job, then my client cannot possibly get a fair hearing," the teachers' union lawyer shot back, proud of being so strategic.

"May I make a statement?" the witness asked. The defeated look she'd worn into the hearing room was gone. Beemer's lawyer's words had ripped it away.

"We were surprised you hadn't asked to already." The chairman smiled at her a little defensively. *The school board knows her.*

When the nurse now spoke, her dignity had its own power. "As you know, I have been a longtime advocate for disability rights. Over the years we have had numerous run-ins." The older board members looked slightly ashamed. The witness turned toward the audience to explain.

"I have always believed that differently abled children are entitled to a public education with their peers. Back when my son was first diagnosed, he was so gravely ill that I had to battle for his right to be educated at all. With the help of the law, and a community of remarkable people fighting with me for those rights, and a board that grew to learn to be responsive, I thought I'd won the war.

"When my son had his heart crushed by that excuse for a man"—she pointed at Beemer but continued before anyone could interrupt—"I am ashamed to say I became bitter. I gave up. After that horrifying day when Mr. Beemer forced him to urinate on himself, my son was mortified. He begged me not to complain to authorities. I took it further. I confessed to the community of advocates who had fought alongside me that I was wrong. Our children did not belong with other children. I internalized what this spiteful, nasty person"—she gestured toward Beemer's lawyer—"just implied, that demeaning a child by calling them 'special needs' is appropriate and justified. I stopped trying to help anyone other than my son and him only in the seclusion of his own home.

"Do you understand? I watched my son begin to disappear and I assisted him." She paused, overcome with shame, but forced herself to resume.

"While I was at work one day my son heard a local news report that this hearing had been scheduled."

Before I could wonder about news coverage the nurse turned unexpectedly to look directly at all of us sitting with Ms. Horne. "He heard about you." She turned toward the audience again. "A group of young men and women brave and good enough to say that the Beemers of this world are wrong. My boy confided, 'Mum, I want to go to school with kids like that.' "

The witness turned back to address the school board. "My son asked me to come here today and tell his story. When I walked in here I was still grieving for what had been taken from me and mine. He"—she pointed at Beemer—"stole something unspeakably precious from us. You"—she pointed at his lawyer—"trying to bully me, you brought it back. I was feeling guilty that I had put my son in such a vulnerable position. I needed you to remind me that anyone can be the target of bullying, not only children with disabilities. My son was right, we *can* take it back." She addressed Beemer: "We cannot allow your viciousness to win." She turned back to the board: "It is *your* responsibility to fix this."

She sat. The audience applauded although they had been warned not to.

When he could regain order the chairman said quietly, "Thank you, madam. We are going to adjourn this hearing for the evening. By the time we resume tomorrow evening I expect you"—he turned to Beemer's lawyer—"to have learned how to behave yourself."

Everyone filed out of the room solemnly. Before she walked over to the nurse, Ms. Horne warned us quietly, "Don't get your hopes up. This is only the beginning. A lot can happen." She had no idea how right she would turn out to be.

Piper's and Sunny's fathers were waiting to drive us home after the hearing. They told us they were proud of us.

36

While the study group was collecting in Dareen's apartment the next afternoon we heard Sunny on the stairs speaking with Dareen's grandmother. *She is so kind to us but still, there is something formidable about her.* "It's for an art project," Sunny explained.

"Naturally," Dareen's grandmother answered, "I will help you." They walked in laden with poster boards, paints, scissors, crayons, glue sticks, fabric scraps, fake flowers, lace, ribbons, buttons, and I couldn't tell how many other endless bits of odds and ends. "Good fight," Dareen's grandmother approved before returning downstairs.

"These are our hearts," Sunny announced, handing a poster board to each of us. "I think we should put whatever we want into them each day of the hearing, OK?"

Rae-Rae looked like she'd been given that horse Sunny and her Gabriel had asked for years ago.

Concentrating on her own poster board, Sunny had a brainstorm. "Ethan's trying to teach me to eat this," she explained, reaching into her backpack and pulling out a package that read,

"Nori." Inside were some ugly brittle sheets of brown stuff that smelled like dead fish.

"Isn't that dried seaweed?" Tia asked.

"It's Beemer's lawyer," Sunny declared.

I broke off a ragged piece, drew a small tombstone on my heart and pasted the Nori inside it.

Rae-Rae opted to draw a little weasel instead.

37

The next two nights there were even more people in the audience. I hoped that was a good sign.

Beemer's student-teacher intern was the first witness on the third day. As she walked over to the microphoned table I realized it had been a long time since I'd seen her. She was dressed simply, in black jeans and a grey-print sweater. I couldn't figure out what made her look different until a Piper fashion observation popped into my head. She was no longer trying to look "teacherly."

"My last assignment before earning my teacher's certificate was to intern for Frederick Beemer. It changed the course of my career. No disrespect to the Adams County District School Board, but I realized that my dream of how education was supposed to happen and the reality of what I observed firsthand were too far apart. My chosen career was untenable."

"It would help if you got to specifics," the chairman advised her. She was young and pretty enough that he softened his tone when he said it.

"Frederick Beemer is an unmitigated bully. I witnessed it every day. He bragged to me about it, attempting to teach me his methods. To my permanent shame, I did nothing to stop him until it almost cost a student his life."

"What do you mean?" Colton Bridgeway leaned forward as he prompted, "That he bragged about it and attempted to teach you his methods?"

"This is only one example: During my first week as his intern he lectured me, 'Listen, little girl: you'll never make it unless you learn how to break their spirits.' He showed me a despicable drawer full of what he called his 'props.' There were several cheap recordable stuffed pigs. When he squeaked one it played 'TH-TH-TH-THAT'S ALL FOLKS!' Mr. Beemer bragged that no one stuttered in *his* classroom. There were fake ICE deportation papers with stickers that read, 'YOU'RE FIRED!' Mr. Beemer laughed at how easy it was to scare what he called 'those Mexicans'—that's what he calls everybody who has any kind of Spanish accent. There were Gideon bibles tabbed to the parts where it supposedly condemns homosexuality, with handwritten post-its that screamed, 'IT'S AN ABOMINATION!'—I never did understand why the LGBTQ students seem to be particularly enraging to Mr. Beemer. He pulled out a bottle of room deodorizer spray, telling me this was one of his favorites. 'Spray this around some kid,' he said, 'and you can cure all those foreign diet and hygiene issues.'

"The drawer was nauseating. It became a representation of what I hated in Mr. Beemer's methods. On my last day, once I knew I had to leave, I took samples from the drawer in case I had to prove what I had seen. I am ashamed I didn't have the courage to do anything with them until the school board contacted me last week."

The witness took several items out of a bookbag she'd carried in with her. The school board lawyer pointed to one of the staff sitting on the sidelines who retrieved them and then hesitated, confused what to do. Following a whispered conference with Mr. Jones, the chairman huffed, "Just hand them to me and I will pass them around."

We all waited in silence while that happened. A few people tittered and then looked ashamed of themselves when one of the board members accidentally squeezed the pig and it stuttered, "Th-th-th-that's all folks."

"I wonder where he got all those bibles," someone behind me leaned over and whispered in my ear.

Mac! I was surprised how glad I was to see him. I guess I'd been worried for him.

Ms. Horne gave him a "be quiet!" look. He muttered, "You can only get them in hotel rooms," before settling himself in the row behind us.

"You never brought your complaints to Frederick Beemer or his superiors?" the chairman asked while the school board lawyer quietly collected and labeled Beemer's "props."

"No, that's not what I meant. I never brought those *items* to anyone," the teacher intern corrected. "I tried repeatedly to raise the issue of bullying with Mr. Beemer but he was insistent that he knew how to teach and I didn't. There were three occasions when I attempted to speak to his superior—the principal—but he was . . . unreceptive." She paused for a moment, debated with herself and then told the chairman: "I have nothing to lose. I might as well be blunt. Do you know what the students call the principal? The Tsar!"

The school board members tried and failed to look shocked.

"He backed all of Mr. Beemer's conduct and blamed my complaints on my lack of experience."

"Did you ever try to complain to any one of us?" an angry-looking board woman seated to the right of the chairman demanded. I'd noticed her last night looking unsympathetic to the testimony. *That's at least one vote against us.*

"I was afraid I would lose my job."

"Why don't you tell us what happened the last day you worked under Frederick Beemer?" Colton Bridgeway hurried to ask.

The student-teacher intern looked like she was about to cry. When a staffer handed her a box of Kleenex she pulled herself together. "I am so ashamed it's difficult for me to get the words out. You have to understand. I still had dreams . . . No, it doesn't matter. During the three and a half weeks I was his intern I witnessed Frederick Beemer repeatedly bring students to tears and beyond. Whatever their perceived vulnerability—social anxiety, language impairment, disability, gender insecurity, *anything*—he and his gang of student lackeys would ridicule them relentlessly. I don't mean a few comments. Once he had someone going he didn't stop. He made one student vomit and then mocked him with gagging sounds for a week afterward—"

"The last day?" the chairman reminded her.

"A student was transferred into one of Mr. Beemer's classes with medical paperwork indicating that because of his epilepsy, he was behind in his schooling and should be brought along slowly in a 'non-stressful environment.' Mr. Beemer seemed to take the student's presence as a personal affront, nicknaming him 'Willy' in a derisive tone and calling upon him more often than any other student. The last day I worked as a teacher, Mr. Beemer summoned that student to the front of the room, forcing the boy to stand before a projected image of his answers from a recent exam. One brave student"—she looked around the room and then pointed to Ethan—"tried to object and was sent to the principal's office. After that interruption, Beemer was worse. He seemed to feel . . . pleasure in causing the student physical distress. By the end of the class, the student's body was unnaturally stiff. He let out a small moan and then his shaking got more pronounced . . . it was horrible ..."

I knew this story but it was still hard to listen.

"When I tried to follow the student out of the classroom, Frederick Beemer ordered me to remain where I was. The first decent act I performed in weeks was to ignore him."

I didn't forgive the teacher intern but I understood her shame. I'd felt the same way: powerless. I only stopped myself from sliding back into that darkness right there in the hearing room by reminding myself that we had some small chance of not being powerless anymore.

The student-teacher intern detailed the rest of the day's events, not even taking comfort in having saved the boy's life when she finally found him, unconscious. By the time she was done, even the angry-looking board woman looked uncomfortable.

A fussy-looking male board member seated close to the chairman asked Beemer's lawyer, "Can you determine for us if your client would be willing to undergo retraining in"—he read from a paper—"the Americans With Disabilities Act, the Individuals with Disabilities Education Act, and the Rehabilitation Act of 1973?"

Mac scoffed contemptuously behind me that the board must have had a training themselves to even know the names of those laws.

"What about retraining on Anti-Discrimination Laws, Title IX, and Anti-Bullying policies?" another overstuffed board member added.

Joshua Jones, the school board attorney, interrupted curtly, cutting off the line of questions: "May I remind you, members of the board, that it is your duty to listen to *all* of the evidence before you find any facts, and that you are not to consider remedies or penalties until after the fact-finding process has been completed."

"He's right!" Beemer's lawyer bragged, deliberately misinterpreting. "I haven't had a chance to cross-examine this witness."

He turned to the student-teacher intern. "Isn't a fact," he roared, "that you made unprofessional and unwanted sexual advances toward Frederick Beemer and when he rejected you, you fabricated this entire story?"

"Don't answer that!" The school board lawyer shot out of his seat. "I am warning you"—Jones turned toward Beemer's attorney—"if you do that again I will file a complaint against you with the Bar Disciplinary Committee. Witnesses in this hearing will be treated with respect. No one will be subjected to discourtesy, let alone baseless slander. You will have some decency, sir."

Pleased with himself, Beemer's lawyer smirked, "In that case, no questions."

"Kindly remain seated," the school board lawyer ordered the witness while he and the chairman whispered back and forth.

Ms. Horne handed Mac a note and sent him off on an assignment she must have considered urgent. "That was deliberate," she hissed beside me. After a moment she wrote me a note too: "Watch Beemer's reactions whenever that tool cross-examines. I'll explain later."

The chairman read out loud from a statement Mr. Jones had scribbled: "With my permission and that of the board"—the chairman turned toward the seated members who dutifully nodded as if they had any clue what they were agreeing to—"our attorney wishes to ask some clarifying questions of this witness."

"My deepest apologies and that of the board for the question you were recently subjected to."

"Thank you."

"When you applied for a student-teaching internship in our school district were you required to submit grades and references?"

"Yes."

"Would you summarize those for us?"

"They were complimentary."

"Aren't you being too humble? Weren't you, for example, in the top 3% academically at your university?"

"Yes."

"And as to your references, would you look at this one and read out loud that middle paragraph, the first sentence?"

"It says, 'I cannot recommend this candidate too highly. She has shown herself to be a model of diligence, accomplishment and integrity.' "

"And these other references, are they similar in tenor?"

"Yes."

"Now, I am going to show you something and ask you if you recognize it."

"It is the phone I purchased when I received my internship."

"Did you use that phone and that phone number for any other purposes?"

"No. I listed that number on all my paperwork with the school and, at Mr. Beemer's insistence, I provided it to him as well."

"After you left your internship did you use that phone for other purposes?"

"No. That phone was only for my work as a student-teacher intern. I'm not sure why I kept it after I left."

"Have you received any calls on that phone recently?"

"Well, you contacted me and we had a few conversations back and forth about me testifying."

"Besides me?"

"I was originally supposed to testify the first night of the hearing. That afternoon I received a voicemail on that phone."

"Would you play that voicemail for us?"

Beemer's attorney shouted, "Objection!" while Mr. Jones walked to the intern to hand her the phone.

Both the chairman and the school board lawyer answered simultaneously, "No objections in this hearing," and the chairman, showing off that he had learned the phrase, added, "The rules of evidence are relaxed."

"Whenever you're ready," Mr. Jones prompted the intern.

When she tapped her phone a tinny but audible voice that sounded very much like Beemer snarled, "Just remember: the accuser can easily become the accused."

Amid audience gasps Mr. Jones asked the witness, "And what was your reaction to that message?"

"It frightened me. I called you and said that I was reconsidering whether I would testify."

"And yet, you are here."

"I failed that boy then. I couldn't live with myself if I failed him again."

. . .

Per instructions from the school board lawyer, the chairman decided to run late and finish with all the testimony about the boy who had almost died. He called Ethan as the next witness.

Ethan looked wobbly approaching the microphoned table but his testimony was flawless, repeating almost word for word what he'd told us that day Beemer sent him to The Tsar. "I am profoundly sorry I could not stop him," Ethan told the board. They didn't ask him anything about being bullied himself. I guessed that would come later. I was wrong.

"Are you familiar with the term LGBTQ?" Beemer's attorney cornered Ethan.

"Somewhat."

"What does the 'Q' stand for?"

"I'm not sure if it's for 'queer' or 'questioning.' "

"Well, which are you?"

While Mr. Jones erupted again, I jotted down on the back of Ms. Horne's note the sequence of questions and then Beemer's snickering loudly when his lawyer asked Ethan, "Which are you?"

Despite Beemer and his lawyer, Ethan finished his testimony with dignity. At the end, he asked if he could add a statement. "Excuse me for being blunt but I still do not understand why my sex life is of concern to my teacher. Or, I might add, to his attorney. When Mr. Beemer thought I was gay, he subjected me to mistreatment. When he realized I had a girlfriend, that treatment altered. What business is that of his? What gives him the right to judge me one way or the other? No matter what sexual orientation I am, I do not think it is appropriate for it to be the grounds for derision, and I cannot believe this board would condone anyone being bullied for it." I was so proud of him.

While Ethan was returning to his seat by us, Rae-Rae slipped her phone out of her bookbag. The chairman had already lectured at length: "All audience cell phones must be turned off." Rae-Rae must have had hers on mute because it made no noise when it sent a prewritten text somewhere.

Before the next witness could be called we heard singing coming from outside the school district building. It sounded like dozens of kids. Thanks to Rae-Rae's schooling us, I recognized the song. Bobby Fuller Four: "I Fought the Law and the Law Won." But those kids had changed the lyrics to: "*You* fought the law and the law won." Toward the end, I heard one voice singing "Fred fought the law and the law won." The next day's local paper had pictures of the protesters with signs that read "Ban the Bully," and others with Beemer's face behind bars. Most of the singers wore rainbows, giving what the newspaper called "new meaning to the term 'gay men's chorus.' "

I expected the board to be cross but they simply waited out the song. Some of them were smiling but most of them tried to keep their faces expressionless.

. . .

To complete what he called corroboration of the student-teacher intern's testimony the chairman called Tia to describe what she'd seen and overheard when the teacher intern rushed in demanding medical attention for an unconscious student.

Beemer's lawyer began his questioning with as much insincerity as he could drip into his words: "As a—oh pardon me. I've been admonished not to use 'offensive language.' " He sneered at Joshua Jones. "As a—is the correct term 'person of color'?—aren't you predisposed to mistrust authority?"

Even while Beemer cackled Tia responded, "Are you saying the color of my skin makes me less credible?" I added to my notes.

"So you admit it."

Tia refused to be bated. "What I learned is that there is a difference between ascribed status and earned status."

Beemer's lawyer tried to ignore her but Colton Bridgeway intervened, asking Tia to explain her answer.

"The way I understand it, all teachers have an ascribed status as soon as they are hired, that comes with the title. But genuine respect, that doesn't come with the job, that has to be earned."

Beemer's lawyer jumped back in, disliking that several board members now looked thoughtful. "You reserve the right to disrespect your teachers!" he accused Tia.

"She just told us about disgraceful conduct she eye-witnessed," Bridgeway angrily interrupted before Tia could respond. "Is it your position, sir, that she should respect your client's right to nearly murder a child?"

Before the hearing got entirely out of his control, the chairman abruptly excused Tia as a witness. Following more of his lawyer's instructions, he called medical personnel concerning the seizure and hospitalization. Beemer literally applauded when his lawyer got a doctor to admit that the boy's epilepsy was long-standing—as if anyone had denied that.

The chairman also called the boy's mother who informed the board, "I don't know why that horrible teacher called my son 'Willy' but that's not his name." At the end, she blurted out, "What I am most sorry about now is that the principal convinced me not to file a complaint. He promised the school would pay the ambulance bill and I couldn't afford to turn him down."

"You were paid off?" Beemer's lawyer asked her. I was running out of room for more notes on my piece of paper.

The chairman issued another "Don't answer that!" instruction. He semi-explained to the mother: "If it were deemed that the seizure was related to misconduct or negligence by the school all costs of emergency treatment would be covered by the school district."

Mac returned with a stack of binder-clipped printouts. The top one said in large bold letters: "**Lawyer's Code of Professional Responsibility.**" Underneath were legal cases that said "**Disciplinary Committee Decision**" on the top of each one. Ms. Horne made a show of handing the stack, titles easily visible, to Joshua Jones.

The chairman announced that testimony would not resume until Monday. By then our hearts were filling up.

38

ADAMS COUNTY HERALD

From the Editor

When Teachers Fail Students

No, we are not talking about grades. This past week the Adams County District School Board heard testimony on a complaint originally generated by students and filed by recently elected School Board Member Colton Bridgeway that Frederick Beemer is the worst kind of classroom bully: a teacher who misuses his authority to degrade, humiliate, and injure the children in his charge.

The testimony thus far–from parents, professionals, and students—has been gut-wrenching. If true, our school board owes it to the children of this district to remove this bully from our school system.

One young man in particular drove this message home. At 20 years old Terrence Cummins has already distinguished himself to the point where he has been granted advanced placement to Purdue University's Masters in Speech Language Pathology program. Fortunately for our community, he will be remaining here until he completes his undergraduate degree and simultaneously will continue his volunteer work for our local Speech Pathology Clinic. What makes his story remarkable is that he is a graduate of that clinic himself.

Terrence Cummins testified that, like many children, he stuttered from his early years on. As he explained, the majority of children outgrow the problem but he was not one of the lucky ones. Over time his stuttering diminished but it had not entirely disappeared when he entered Adams High School. Anxiety and stress in particular would worsen his symptoms. Shockingly, so did Frederick Beemer, according to Terrence Cummins's testimony.

As did other students with speech difficulties who had suffered in Beemer's class, Terrence described a course of bullying by Teacher Beemer that included taunts, humiliation, and mockery. A separate witness who had been Beemer's teaching assistant produced a stuffed Porky Pig that she testified this so-called "teacher" employed to torment students. Terrence Cummins confirmed that Beemer would end a session of mimicry by squeezing the toy until it said "Th-th-th-that's all folks!" The boy told the school board members that because he was distraught at this treatment and the ridicule of his teacher and fellow students, he stopped speaking altogether. School records confirm that Terrence's official transcript when he graduated included the notation "elective mutism."

Once freed of the destructive effects of Frederick Beemer's reign of terror, the boy overcame his disability and dedicated his life to helping others similarly afflicted. As inspiring as his life story is, it is disgraceful that our county permitted this maltreatment to be inflicted by a public employee on a student in our schools. Most horrifyingly, Terrence's shocking narrative was only one of many. Our excuse before now was that we did not know. Now that we do, our choice is: we must act or be complicit. It is time to let the Adams County District School Board know that sadistic bullying will not be tolerated from any member of our district's faculty.

39

Ms. Horne's "I'll-explain-later" session happened Monday afternoon in the courthouse between her cases. I loved her idea so much she had to caution me: "I don't know if he'll give you this opportunity or not. Don't reach for it if it's not there—it has to come out naturally. But I think he's that arrogant a fool that you'll get your chance."

Monday night's session was unexpectedly canceled. We used the time at the dojo calling out "Threat!" and attacking the pads.

Tuesday at school some students we didn't know fist-bumped us. Even if it turned out to be only temporary, Beemer on leave and The Tsar closeted in his office made the school feel like the air was cleaner. The one shadow was that I kept expecting Berry to confront me again, defending Beemer, but she didn't seem to be around either.

· · ·

Mr. Jones, the school board lawyer, started Tuesday night's session announcing that he had some statements to read for the record. The first was from a psychiatric social worker:

"I am currently counseling a mother and her adolescent son who have requested that I prepare this report concerning their therapy and submit it to the Adams County District School Board. In my records are their signed consents which confirm that they have made this request. They wish to avoid the personal trauma testifying might entail for them and they wish to protect their identities.

"The boy insists upon being called 'Squeaky' and will be so referenced in this report at his request although that name appears nowhere in his records nor on his birth certificate.

"The child was born with spina bifida which at this point requires him to use a wheelchair. Prior to his being mainstreamed in Adams High School his mother reports that he had adapted well to wheelchair use and had no extraordinary complaints concerning it. The boy concurs with this assessment although he adds, 'It's because I didn't know.'

"The boy reports that he has a teacher he refers to as 'Mr. Beemer.' He credits that teacher with being 'the only one honest enough to tell me the truth.' The mother reports that this teacher has convinced her child that his wheelchair squeaks. Hence the nickname 'Squeaky.' The mother insists that the wheelchair has never squeaked. Nevertheless, she took it in for repairs and had the technicians prepare a report that it is in perfect working condition. This report has not convinced the boy.

"Therapy for this family presents a delicate and difficult challenge. The boy is unprepared to believe that his teacher could be so cruel as to deceive him or that his classmates are secretly laughing at him. Leading him to those truths, if it can be accomplished at all, entails a severe risk of harm to his otherwise impressive adjustment to his disability.

"Let me be clear: apparently for his own entertainment, the teacher has convinced this child it would be insane to believe his wheelchair does not squeak. The child cannot win—either he adopts this falsehood or he is crazy. The child chose the less painful of these two alternatives. I find the conduct of this teacher reprehensible and shocking. I have enclosed several articles on 'gaslighting' as that term is used clinically, which I believe demonstrate that the teacher's behavior is a classic form of bullying. It may not be my place to say, but my personal opinion is that it is incumbent on the Adams County District School Board to prevent such conduct in the future."

After he read that Mr. Jones, looking extremely angry, entered into the hearing record a signed affidavit from an attorney for Adams County Family Services:

"We are in possession of a number of subpoenas from an individual claiming to represent one Frederick Beemer in a disciplinary hearing before the Adams County District School Board. Those subpoenas request child protective and foster care records of potential witnesses at that hearing. We consider those subpoenas illegal and unconscionable. The mere fact that there may well be extensive records of children within our jurisdiction does not deprive those children of the privacy rights accorded other children fortunate enough not to need our services. We have no intention of honoring these subpoenas and consider them to be a legal nullity. Should this board require my personal presence, or should this teacher's lawyer seek to litigate the issue, my legal address for service of process appears at the bottom of this affidavit."

With a lot less confidence than his lawyer, the chairman then read a board statement into the record:

"We do not require the presence of the Adams County Family Services attorney and we will not be granting an adjournment of this hearing for the issue to be litigated."

Finally, the board was ready to listen to testimony. Besides Ethan and Tia describing the day they'd seen a student almost die, none of us from OBaaT had been called to the microphoned table. We were expecting it.

. . .

Jade was the first. The closed-off look she'd worn for most of the past year was gone, replaced with a kind of steely, defiant determination. *She's done this before.*

"Because I'm a Spanish speaker, I was present for the interviews of the ESL students. I have their permission to summarize what they confided in me. The saddest of them, at least to me, was a Puerto Rican kid about my age. Like me, he is light-skinned. You may not know this but there is a great deal of color-consciousness among Latino people. Being lighter-skinned is considered . . . desirable, which makes darker kids resent them. This boy I'm talking about had tried very hard to be accepted but he wasn't from Central or South America and he didn't look like anyone else in his ESL classes. He had a tough time of it."

"Tough how?" Colton Bridgeway asked her. He knew our report—he'd seen it before any other board member—so I guessed his questions were all designed to bring out the parts that he felt were strongest.

"I think one of the ugliest concepts ever is shunning. I studied it. Do you know when an animal gets ostracized they often die? But with animals, it's behavior-based. If a wolf is too aggressive for the pack, the other wolves may banish him to preserve the group. It's only humans that banish someone for no good reason at all. It doesn't have to be something they do, only something they *are*." She brushed away the tear rolling down her cheek as if she was angry at it. "That's what happened with this kid. He was all alone."

When Jade had started to explain, the board had kind of shifted in their seats like, "Get to the point." But they were listening by the time she finished.

"What was it that happened with this boy?" Bridgeway asked.

"Mr. Beemer is what happened. I don't know how isolated the kid might have wound up anyway but when Beemer found out—he didn't even know this!—that Puerto Ricans are US citizens and cannot be deported, I think he was frustrated he couldn't use the same kind of intimidation he had with other Spanish speakers. In front of everyone, he started telling the kid, 'You know you're not one of them, don't you? No way you're not white. The people you think are your parents must have kidnapped you.' That boy loves his parents. Beemer's words would have been hurtful all by themselves. What made it much worse is that what Beemer said—besides being cruel and ignorant—was all the excuse the other students needed. They started acting like the kid didn't exist. They wouldn't speak to him. They wouldn't let him sit with them at lunch. He was a total, cold-and-alone outcast.

"Every time there was any kind of thaw, Beemer would start in again. 'Lose that Spanish accent. That's the language of your kidnappers.' When I interviewed him, I think I was the first student who'd spoken to him in Spanish in months. He didn't have any friends to begin with. I may have been the first kid who'd spoken to him at all. In any language. Can you understand how that must hurt? To be hated for nothing you've done wrong? Nothing you can change?"

"Was this boy the only Spanish speaker who told you about being bullied by Frederick Beemer?" Colton Bridgeway asked.

"Oh no. He was the one who got to me most but nearly all of them repeated taunts and threats from Mr. Beemer, mostly about their English deficiencies—whether they had them or not—and their immigration status or the status of people they were worried about."

While Jade repeated the specifics I studied her. Her testimony was precise and strong. Stronger than I thought I could be. But underneath there was something . . . grieving. Until the cross-examination. That's when I understood it was not only my records Joshua Jones had protected.

When it was his turn, Beemer's attorney jumped up out of his seat, waved the complaint at Jade, and accused, "None of these people exist, do they? You made it all up!"

"What are you *talking* about?"

"These names. There's no one at my client's school with any of those names! Admit it!"

Jade gave him a "you're-a-moron" look and answered, "It says right in the complaint, those are pseudonyms. You know, made-up names to protect identity. We told the school board from the very start that we would withhold the real names of anyone whose immigration status might be questioned. The school board agreed to hear their accounts through us."

"But you gave *your* name, didn't you?"

"Yes."

"You think you're above the law? You think—" When the school board attorney started to stand, Beemer's lawyer decided not to finish the next question. Instead, he repeated, "You think you're above the law?"

"I am not at risk of being deported like the people I interviewed."

"Because"—Beemer's lawyer glanced at the school board attorney—"you're special?"

"Because I was born here. Of parents who were born here. I am as much a citizen as you are."

"Now that you mention your parents—" Beemer's lawyer started as if that was where he'd intended to go all along.

"—No!" the school board lawyer shouted. "You were warned, explicitly and in writing, to stay away from that topic. A topic"—Mr. Jones turned to address his clients, the school board itself—"that has nothing to do with this hearing and entails a grave risk of harm." Turning back to Beemer's lawyer: "You're done. No more questions of this witness. You sacrificed that right."

. . .

Beemer's lawyer muttered something about "appellate remedies." Ignoring him, Mr. Jones escorted Jade back to her seat and immediately called Rae-Rae as a witness, skipping the step where he whispered to the chairman and the chairman called the witness.

None of us had time to think about what had just happened with Jade before Rae-Rae, in answer to a bunch of questions, summarized her interviews with the LGBTQ community. She repeated what we'd heard so often, that the gay kids were convinced that Beemer targeted them more than anyone else. "I don't know why," Rae-Rae added, which I think gave her even more credibility.

"Was there one interview in particular that stood out for you?" Colton Bridgeway asked her with a smile, proving he *had* done his homework when he'd reviewed our report before sharing it with the other board members.

"Oh yes!" Rae-Rae chirped happily. "There was one boy—I'm not going to name him if that's OK?—who Beemer had privately threatened to out. The boy is the . . . well he is a very recognized athlete at our school. He's all-state and he's gotten big offers for college scholarships and I guess Mr. Beemer thought he had some power over him. But the boy answered Mr. Beemer in front of all his teammates and everyone that he was *already* out. He made no secret of being gay. When the boy said that, all his teammates cheered. After that, Mr. Beemer didn't speak to anyone on the team at all."

When it was his turn, Beemer's lawyer tried to use the boy as proof that Beemer's words were not all that harmful. Rae-Rae stood right up to him: "You're saying no harm, no foul? Let me tell you, sir, 'only the strong survive' is not supposed to be a high school motto."

"No more questions," Beemer's lawyer backed away. All of a sudden we were done for the night.

Jade tried to avoid getting a ride home with us until I whispered her a promise that no one would ask her any questions.

40

The next day in creative writing Mrs. Harbinger announced that she had a special in-class assignment:

"This project is not for credit. It will not be graded or go toward any 'extra credit' accounting. It is entirely voluntary.

"All of you by now are aware that the Adams County District School Board is conducting a hearing and that several students in this class have a role in it. My suggestion is that those of you who wish to engage in this exercise write a one-page poem, story, or statement about that fact.

"You may submit the papers to me either anonymously or under your signature entirely at your discretion. You may consider it as simply an exercise in perfecting your skills or as a way to express your opinions. Obviously, those students in OBaaT— the students who are participating in the hearing—are exempt from this assignment and they and any of you who decline this exercise may use this period to work on your end-of-semester creative writing projects.

"Any of you who do wish to participate, please hand your papers to me at the end of class. I will review them, give you writing feedback if you wish it, and then deliver them to OBaaT. You are free to express whatever thoughts or ideas you choose as long as they are content-appropriate."

There had been a steady buzz of reaction throughout Mrs. Harbinger's long announcement. At the end, when she used the phrase "content-appropriate" several of my classmates laughed but it didn't sound mean.

. . .

We waited until we were all at Sunny's that night, early enough before the hearing to have time to ourselves. Then we opened the manila envelope Mrs. Harbinger had given us and started passing around what the other kids in our creative writing class had to say.

Rae-Rae was the first to react, gleeful: "You have to hear this one!

"I think you're nuts
But you've got guts
So kick some butts!"

One classmate wrote a page called "Silent Witness":

"When I first heard about OBaaT I thought to myself that they were Don Quixote tilting at modern windmills. I thought that bullying is just the way things are. However, over time I've come to believe that they are right and I was wrong. My complaisance"—(Mrs. Harbinger had circled the word with a suggestion that a simpler word would work better)—"permitted me to witness bullying and say nothing. I thought if I wasn't the bully or someone supporting him out loud then I wasn't part of the problem. That was a convenient excuse to do nothing. I only

197

realized that when someone I thought of as a friend asked me how to get in touch with OBaaT. I never knew he was bullied. I understand now that is because I never wanted to know. My silence was not neutral. It made my friend's hurt worse because he thought I didn't care. Now I have promised myself I will be

'Silent No More.' "

There were lots of notes congratulating us and cheering us on. Then when we were no longer prepared for it, one totally sobering one:

"Please don't try to find me. You don't know me and if I have my way you never will. Frederick Beemer ruined my life. I hope you ruin his."

41

The Tsar was in the audience when we walked into the hearing room. His self-importance looked pasted on.

There was a long delay while we waited for the board to file in. When they finally did the chairman said something that made me feel cheated and let off the hook at the same time. He announced: "We have been conferring and have come to the determination that we have heard sufficient evidence to make our determination—"

"—Wait a minute!" Beemer's lawyer yelled. "I have witnesses. You can't—"

"—I was just about to get to that," the chairman cut him off, annoyed by the interruption. He read from a paper obviously prepared by the school board lawyer. "Frederick Beemer, please be advised that you have the right to testify yourself or call any relevant witnesses. You should also be advised that you are under no obligation to do so."

Without bothering to respond, Beemer's lawyer called The Tsar to testify. The principal must have thought it looked more dignified to give a speech standing up but he had to practically shout toward the microphone on the table.

"I pride myself on running a tight ship. One of the most valuable members of my crew, as it were, is Frederick Beemer. The fact that he is not the most popular teacher at my school is, in my opinion, a mark in his favor not against it. Let me tell you, ladies and gentlemen, this whole sorry affair, the witch hunt of a complaint that led to this hearing, is about popularity and not substance. Some students with agendas of their own cooked this up. I understand that you are obligated to listen to what they have to say, but that does not mean you should believe it. I am in a position to know the truth more than any of you possibly can. And I say what these students"—he waved his hands toward us—"put on paper is an offensive mixture of innuendo, exaggeration and outright lies. You"—this time he turned to face us directly—"should be ashamed of yourselves."

As the Tsar seated himself, the school board lawyer was writing furiously. When he handed the paper to the chairman everyone in the room could see that Mr. Jones ordered, "Read it."

The chairman rose and announced, "Sir, you are specifically advised that this board will not tolerate any retaliation against any student or witness in this hearing. If we receive any complaints of"—he pointed to a word that his lawyer recited phonetically to him—" 'retaliatory' conduct, it is you who will find yourself before this board." The chairman glanced at his lawyer for confirmation before sitting back down.

Mr. Jones asked The Tsar: "Is that understood?"

"Yes."

"Do you have any direct knowledge of any incident listed in the district school board complaint against Frederick Beemer?"

"No direct knowledge, no."

"Sir, you are excused."

The Tsar left the hearing room. To me, it seemed like he was trying to look victorious but it was unconvincing.

. . .

The teacher's union attorney was ready to call his next witness. We all expected Beemer to testify but instead, his lawyer called . . . my name. I looked at Ms. Horne. She gave me an encouraging, sympathetic smile. Hoke's hand touched my arm for reassurance. I wondered if I looked wobbly like Ethan walking over to the microphoned table. I sure felt it.

"OBat was your idea wasn't it."

"I thought up the name, yes."

"Organization of Batgirls."

"Excuse me?"

"Oh come on, Anna. Admit it, that's what OBat stands for."

"No. I've never even heard of a 'batgirl.'" *Oops, don't volunteer.*

"You know. Don't you all dress up as batgirls for Halloween? Some feminist comic book hero?"

"You mean Wonder Woman?" People were laughing in the audience. I was so nervous I flashed on a mental picture of Wonder Squirrel Woman and had to warn myself not to get distracted. "I think maybe there was a Batwoman TV show."

"What do *you* claim OBat stands for?"

"O.B.a.a.T. One Bully at a Time."

"You admit Frederick Beemer was always the target for you and your girl gang." *Didn't he just concede Beemer was a bully?*

"No."

"You're like the pack leader, right? He gave you or one of your little pals a bad grade and you had it in for him, didn't you."

"He never gives us girls bad grades." The words were out of my mouth before I could stop them. *Only say what you can document.* Fortunately, Beemer's lawyer didn't want to go there any more than I did.

"Let's get back to OBaaT. If it wasn't all about attacking this one innocent teacher, who else did you accuse of being a bully?"

"The first thing OBaaT did was befriend a girl who was being beaten up by her foster father."

"So you claim."

"No, the authorities decided."

"You got someone to lie about their own foster father?!"

"The school called in the report based on all her bruises. The police arrested him. After that, we offered to be her friends."

"And now, coincidence of coincidences, she's one of the people accusing Frederick Beemer of being a bully."

"No. She doesn't live here anymore. She got a scholarship to art school in Chicago."

"Admit it, she's one of your so-called interviews."

"All the students who told us about Mr. Beemer bullying them were boys." *Why do we keep winding up back here? At least this time I can back it up.*

Beemer's lawyer switched gears. "You, all of you Batgirls, you don't like authority much, do you?"

"I don't know what that question means."

"Well, look at you all." *He's sneering at my friends!* "That one looks like a Muslim and—"

A board member sitting on the end opposite our friend Colton Bridgeway interrupted, very angry: "Just what are you saying about the Muslim religion, sir?" He worded it like a question but it sounded like a threat.

"No, no, no!" the chairman intervened, glancing nervously toward the table crowded with reporters. "I apologize, Dr. Aziz. That question should never have been asked and it will not be answered. Frederick Beemer, I would suggest you advise your lawyer that such slurs only harm your cause."

Beemer's lawyer looked over at the union representative seated in the back. The representative shook his head no. The lawyer shrugged.

"May I say something?" I asked as demurely as I could, looking up at the table of board members.

The chairman reluctantly agreed.

I turned back to Beemer's lawyer. "I know you are trying to goad me by insulting my friends. But we're not the villains here. You picked on Dareen. Do you know what her name means? You're right, it's Arabic—it's that beautiful moment when a flower first opens. Jade, she's a precious stone, right? But it's not our names or how we look that count here. It's what we do. You want to say we did it out of hate but we didn't. We did it because we hated seeing kids hurt."

"Isn't it true that you think anyone you don't like is a bully?"

"No."

"You think I am a bully, don't you."

"I think you hurt people on purpose."

"You're admitting it, you're calling me a bully."

"I think you are deliberately cruel as a strategy. That's different than what a bully does."

"A strategy!" Beemer's lawyer was blustering now. "What strategy could I possibly have?"

"I think you're trying to make meanness seem normal. I think you want to distract this board"—I looked at them earnestly like my lawyer had taught me—"from the truly awful truth, that Mr. Beemer, he *enjoys* causing pain. It would have worked better if your client hadn't laughed every time you hurt anyone's feelings in this courtroom." *Not a courtroom. That was dumb.*

Beemer's lawyer rose from his seat, advanced toward me snarling, "Very fancy thinking, little girl. Who told you to say that nonsense?" He kept asking questions without waiting for answers until he asked the next one I'd been hoping for: "How come if I'm so mean, that's not me bullying you? Are you immune from—"

"—You can't bully me because you have no authority over me. Mr. Beemer, he picks out the kids least able to defend themselves and deliberately injures them deep inside. All you've done is offend some people who volunteered to be drafted. You can be as cruel as you want, talk about me being a foster kid—that's why you wanted my foster records, right? You think you'll find dirt on me. What you say, it's just words. Some kids get destroyed by words but you, you have no power here. These people"—I looked directly at the board again like I'd been taught—"are here to protect me. Mr. Beemer, he is our *teacher*. We have no protection from him. We all know he has the backing of the principal. There's all sorts of ways he can make us pay for defying him—"

By then the lawyer was shouting over my words. Still, I would have gone on but everybody could see I was getting upset. Colton Bridgeway took that as a cue to step in.

"Do you have any specific questions of this witness, who *you* called, or do you solely want to badger her?"

"I'm done with her," Beemer's lawyer shot back, trying to make it sound like a win. *My true family thinks he's wrong.* Back in his seat, he looked a hard question at his client who shook his head vehemently "no."

"No further witnesses."

"Then the evidence portion of this hearing is concluded," the chairman read the words written for him by the school board lawyer. "We will retire—"

"—Wait a minute! My client has the right to make a final statement."

"I thought you said—"

"—No, he does not wish to testify. He will not subject himself to what may well be hostile interrogation." Beemer's lawyer shot Bridgeway and Jones accusatory glares. "Nevertheless he has the right—"

"—Frederick Beemer," the school board attorney cut to the chase, "what statement do you wish to make?"

Beemer's chair creaked as he rose and screeched on the floor as he cleared space to speak expansively. "I want to say that I am one hundred percent innocent." *That's not even original!* As ceremoniously as he'd risen, he sat back down again.

At a nod from Mr. Jones, the chairman resumed reading: "We will retire to deliberate. A written decision will be forthcoming within approximately two weeks' time."

That suddenly, it was done. My friends hugged me. Ms. Horne found a private place to tell us, "No matter the outcome—and I can't begin to guess what the board will decide—you all did beautiful, brave work. You deserve to know when you look in the mirror that a hero is looking back."

42

The day it all happened we were at Dareen's. We'd tried studying but it seemed like the long, tense days of waiting for the school board's decision had eaten into our ability to concentrate. Sunny's poster board hearts were stacked in a corner, unfinished. Even trying to plan for the Rescues Rule! Festival coming up in a month felt more like an obligation than fun.

This morning during second period the assistant principal's voice had interrupted class to announce an administrative and staff meeting. Normal classes had ended at noontime. We'd all headed here to Dareen's by default, but now we were not quite sure why. When we'd shed our jackets and sweaters we'd left them in a pile around us because it felt like too much trouble to put them away. Normally we were neat, disciplined. Not today.

Even Piper was dressed down—in crumpled grey sweats. She'd come in late, looking drained. As soon as she had dumped her book bag and shawl, she'd reached for her cell phone and pressed the mute button. Still, for the past hour, it had been flashing every few minutes. She punched the "ignore" button so often she eventually powered down the phone. That's why hers was the only one that didn't ping when we all got a group text from Ms. Horne: "Meet at my office at 5:45 p.m. There may be news."

The energy in the room surged in an instant. Our wildest speculations turned out to be not half as improbable as the truth, but we couldn't have known that then. If we hadn't been distracted—at least that's what I tell myself now—things might not have gotten as out of hand.

. . .

In the midst of our chatter, Dareen's grandmother knocked on the door. *It's her apartment.* "I apologize for the interruption but he says it is *urgent.*" Turning to someone behind her, Dareen's grandmother raised all her fingers for emphasis: "Ten minutes." *Hoke is still in class. It must be Ethan with news!* But it wasn't.

Piper's boyfriend Lance stood in the doorway, weeping. "It's OK," Piper told Dareen who reluctantly stepped aside to let Lance in.

"Lance, I told you. It's over. There's nothing to discuss."

"You can't mean that, Piper. We were destined to be together. I know you only said different because your father forced you to."

Piper drew herself up. "No one forced me. My dad doesn't force me and you don't either. This is my decision and you are not going to change my mind."

That quick, Lance transformed. You could see it. Meek one second, lethal the next. I didn't know he could look so . . . blood-chilling.

"That's the way it is?"

Piper saw it too but she still forced herself to say, "Yes."

Jade had hit "record" on her cell almost as soon as Lance had walked in. Now I saw her tilt her phone toward him. I saw Sunny move to stand beside Piper in an I've-got-your-back posture. I saw Tia and Dareen face off to Lance, backing closer to Piper. It was the way I'd seen pit bulls with their fangs bared edge back toward one of their own when it needed defending. I saw Rae-Rae start forward to Lance. I have no idea if I moved at all. Lance was deadly still.

"You know I can't let that happen Piper. You don't get to leave me. That's not allowed."

What made Lance's voice truly frightening was that it was perfectly calm. Reciting self-evident facts. Not a threat, an inevitability. "First," he said to himself methodically, "we have to do something about that pretty face."

In my mind now I can see all the individual pieces of the sequence although I know they all happened at once. Lance pulled a spray bottle from his pocket, at the same time that Jade moved closer to him with her phone camera, at the same time that Piper tried to shield her face with her arms while she cringed away from his weapon, at the same time that Lance spun, lunging at Jade and her phone, at the same time that someone I later found out was me screamed "*Threat*!" at the same time that thankfully all our months of training kicked in. Grabbing jackets and coats and book bags we all swarmed Lance together, one moving multi-bodied force.

There was a heart-stopping moment after the clash and clatter when we were all down but I didn't know if it had worked. Near me, I heard a sizzle and watched the liquid from the bottle Lance had dropped burn a hole in the carpet. We'd stunned

Lance and he'd fallen—down and hopefully unarmed—but not out. When Lance started to rise we were ready for him but by then Dareen's grandmother was at the door again, a meat cleaver in her hand.

"Get out. You will leave, now, and you will not return." It was hard not to gasp at the lethal seriousness in the older woman's steel-edged voice.

"You're dead, Piper," Lance hissed at her. Then to all of us: "You're all dead." Eyeing the hatchet, he headed down the stairs, Dareen's grandmother following grimly behind him. Out of nowhere though, there was turmoil coming *up* the stairs.

The momentum of the two uniformed police officers pounding toward us reversed Lance and Dareen's grandmother's direction. In some recess of my mind I registered Dareen's mother right behind the cops. In one fluid movement, she slid the meat cleaver out of her mother's hand and flowed soundlessly into the kitchen where I could half-see her incongruously arranging a whole raw chicken on a cutting board next to the implement. Amid the chaos in the living room, I didn't notice her again until she calmly reminded her mother that someone needed to admit walk-in patients and would she unlock the doors and do that.

By then Lance was in handcuffs, swearing, spitting and kicking at the big angry-looking cop who was taunting him: "I knew you'd never make it on probation, punk. I told that judge, 'Anyone who would beat up a bum that bad and set him on fire, they were plain evil.' The judge wanted to give you 'one last chance.' Looks like you used that up." An ugly laugh came out of the cop but it didn't make me feel sorry for Lance.

Then Lance made me hate him more by pleading, "Piper, tell them it's all a misunderstanding. I love you. I could never hurt you. Tell them you won't press charges."

Piper asked, "Officer, are there papers I need to sign?" almost at the same time that Rae-Rae got up in Lance's face.

"We were all here, you dipwad."

. . .

"And we have it on tape, full audio and video," said one of the three police who now entered the room. They weren't in uniform but all three of them were wearing gold badges on chains around their necks.

"You sure you're all right?" one of them was asking but it wasn't Piper the question was directed to . . . it was Jade.

"I'm sorry, Detective. I must have hit the button when he"— she shrugged toward Lance as if he was a cockroach—"tried to grab the phone."

"Jade, how many times have I told you, if you're ever in danger I'll be here."

"Thank you, Detective," she whispered.

"And how many times I gotta tell you to call me Ed?

"You picked the wrong targets, kid," Ed informed Lance. He nodded at the uniformed officers to take Lance to jail.

Piper called her dad to cancel their arrangements for him to pick her up and to update him on the Lance situation. She downplayed what had happened so he wouldn't worry.

We were all quiet—I think maybe we were in shock—while the three detectives photographed what they called the "crime scene." They used special gloves to gingerly pick up the spray bottle and place it in a glass jar one of them labeled and stored in her gear.

"Ma'am," Ed apologized to Dareen's mother, "we need to cut a piece of your carpet and the padding underneath it where the acid burned through. Perhaps you have surgical scissors we could borrow. That hatchet"—he slipped in his reassurance with a straight face—"is probably too blunt. I'm sorry to put you to the trouble but I'll give you all the paperwork you need to apply to crime victims' compensation for repayment of your costs of repair."

"Certainly, Detective," Dareen's mom answered him, formally but not ungraciously.

As politely, the three detectives interviewed each of us and took our statements and contact information. They gave Piper their cards, the crime report number, and follow-up instructions for the criminal complaint. Before they left Ed turned to Jade and said softly, "I hope things are better at—" but she shook her head to cut him off. He amended it to "—I hope you're OK."

After the door closed and she was assured we were finally alone, Dareen's mom comforted us: "You girls have been through a lot. I suspect you can help each other more than anyone else can help you. I'll leave you to yourselves for now but if you want anything, all you have to do is ask. We will be right downstairs." *No formality. That must be only for strangers.* She caught my eye before she left the room, mimed butchering a chicken, and joked: "Good alibi, huh?" before she winked at me. Bowing to her daughter she murmured, "justice girl," in an affirmation of Dareen that was breathtakingly beautiful.

· · ·

As soon as the door closed leaving us gratefully alone, our lovely Piper started to tremble. More to herself than to us, she whispered, "I was so scared" over and over as if repeating it could make the feeling go away.

Jade, her angles sharper than ever, crouched in front of Piper. She put her palms together in an unconscious prayer gesture and chanted mournfully, "Please don't hate me, please don't hate me, please don't hate me."

Piper didn't react right away. I think it must have taken a while before Jade's voice penetrated that dark, alone place. When it did Piper looked at Jade, shocked. "How could I hate you? I love you. And besides, you saved me. What would make you think such a crazy thing?"

She sat Jade next to her on the couch, arms wrapped around her, Piper's tearful grey-clothed grace not softening Jade's black, ragged edges.

A moment and then Piper's brief strength dissolved. "I'm the one you should all hate." She looked around at the disheveled bunch of us and the upended room. "I was sure, if I was only strong enough, I could do what I needed to. But I should never have told you, Dareen, that it was OK to let Lance in. I'd already told him it was over, in front of my dad. Then when Lance kept texting me and I ignored it and then he showed up here, I thought if I said it in front of all of you, it would finally take. But I had no right to put you all"—she gasped—"at risk. I'm sorry. I'm so, so sorry."

"No!" Dareen contradicted. "All that work: this, right here is why we did it. Don't you apologize. You made us proud."

"I need to explain," Piper non-answered. "Rae-Rae, do you remember when you were testifying and you said 'Not everyone is strong'?" Out of Piper's line of vision, Rae-Rae shook her head to my silent question. Neither one of us thought Rae-Rae had used those words. "I felt like a fraud, standing against somebody else's bully as long as all of you were beside me, but in private letting Lance ..."

"What if he'd caught you alone! Before, did he—" Rae-Rae started to ask but Piper cut her off.

"—No, he never hit me. Can you understand people can be frightening without ever touching you?"

"Yes," Jade mouthed the word. Piper hugged her closer.

"Before I knew him, I remember thinking Lance was so hot—in that almost-but-not-dangerous kind of way. That's so embarrassing to admit now. But once we were a thing, I couldn't have described what he looked like. It was as if the emotions—his and mine—were painted into the air, blocking out my vision. Most of the time, I felt like I couldn't see."

Piper wiped at her eyes. Before we could fill the pause with reassurances she continued, "No, I know you all want to tell me it wasn't my fault. Anyone can misjudge a person. But . . . I couldn't find a way out."

"Explain why, Piper." I shouldn't have said it so bossy, especially since I thought I knew the answer. I wanted her to know it, to repeat what she'd told Ms. Horne until it stayed in her consciousness. But she didn't.

"You know how you see someone and it starts out good and then it isn't and at some point you say to yourself 'Well this isn't working' and you both agree to move on?" Piper almost smiled as she asked us. "It's like we all have this unspoken understanding that anyone can end it. Lance, he said it was *his* decision whether he would let me go. That I had no say." She shuddered. "Not being able to stop him, that's what I couldn't admit to myself . . . or to all of you. I let—" Piper interrupted herself. "Jade, do you remember I tried to ask you after Health Education one day, why you thought women stay with someone who hurts them?"

There was something strangled in Jade's voice as she answered, "Yes."

"I was afraid I was one of them."

"You're nothing like that!" Jade almost snapped at Piper. "Maybe early on you felt sorry for him, or you doubted your decision or whatever. Anybody could do that. But you never took his side against anyone else." *Where did that come from?*

"It still feels like if I only hadn't been weak—"

"—You're not weak, Piper," Jade insisted. "I won't let you believe that. I know what weak looks like. And selfish, and you're none of that."

"Piper!" I paused but I forced myself to go on no matter how hard my own words hurt me: "Remember when Willy had his seizure and that didn't even stop Beemer? I couldn't stand that I'd failed all of you. I was so ashamed that I hid from my own family. It was Charity who taught me—Beemer is *our* fight, not *my* fight. So is Lance."

"This war we joined," Tia seconded me, "it was always about us, Piper. We wanted to find a way to stand with each other. Now that we have, don't take that away from us with an 'I'm sorry.' "

"You let us in when you were ready," Dareen added, her next words sounding like a mantra: "Timing is neutral, with its own rhythm. The honor is in doing battle."

"Besides, you are the one who started this fight of ours. Don't you remember?" Rae-Rae asked her. "We were in the girls room and Lance knocked on the door, saying you were his ..."

"I've been afraid so long . . ." Piper shuddered. "And now"—a tiny flash of brightness in her face—"I'm not."

"That's right," Sunny picked up. "You gave us a gift, Piper. You being brave enough to face Lance today, it was what we all needed to help you. Back in that girls room, I felt helpless. Now I don't. You did that."

"I should feel proud?" Piper asked doubtfully.

"Yes!" we all shouted.

"What made us angry enough to start OBaaT, it was being worried about you, Piper," Sunny continued. "And Ethan, before I knew him. And Charity when we still called her 'the new girl.' And you, Jade—" Sunny interrupted herself to add, "But I was wrong to push you."

"No." Jade let the words reluctantly out of her mouth: "I have to be as brave as Piper. I . . . I owe you all an explanation."

Finally

43

"Wait," Piper interrupted. *Jade needing her is making her stronger.* She unwrapped her arms from Jade, turned to face her, and took Jade's hands in her own. "I want you to know that"—Piper's eyes asked and received permission from all of us to perform our ceremony—"I will always love you and you will always be family."

Dareen looked like she might bow but held Jade's hands instead. "You saved us all. I will always love you and you will always be family."

I took Jade's hands next. "Lilly-Belle loves you the same way I do—wholly. Not unconditionally, but for who you are. Nothing you tell us will change that I will always love you and you will always be family."

Rae-Rae quoted Roy Orbison: " 'Only the lonely know this feeling ain't right.' I know. I will always love you and you will always be family."

Sunny promised, "We all want to fight whatever is hurting you so. But no matter whether you let us, I will always love you and you will always be family."

Tia ended it, non-parliamentarian. "There's no one set of rules for being friends and sisters. We know you are not capable of doing anything shameful the same way we know that about Piper. If you tell us, whatever you do or don't tell us, we will always love you and you will always be family."

We waited for Jade to say the words herself. "I know I will always love you and you will always be family."

It was only because we protested that she changed it. It was visibly hard for her to get the words out: "I know you will always love me and you will always be family."

We settled into hushed listening positions. Jade started her story talking to the far wall but after a while she talked directly to us.

. . .

"My father, my *real* father, was a good, loving man. He made me feel like I was his whole world, always surrounding me with affection. It was like he was delighted with everything I said and did and was. You probably think four years old is too young to remember that kind of thing and it's true I don't remember specifics, but I will never forget the way he made me feel.

"After he died, it was only me and my mother. Because of the way it is now, it's hard to think that she was kind to me back then but she must have been even after it was only the two of us. I know I must have believed she loved me or I wouldn't have been so shocked when it was gone.

"For years after my dad died she dated off and on but nothing serious. I was nine when she met and married my stepfather." Hatred darkened Jade's face. "I *never* liked him but it wasn't as if he abused me or anything. Back then he didn't hit my mother either. That came when I started . . . well when I hit puberty. He would stare at me, at my almost nonexistent breasts and hips.

"He and my mother began clashing over me and that's when he started beating up on her. He never hit me but if he big-eyed me too much, she would. Hers to me were only slaps but his to her were full-on punching and kicking. It seems like each time was worse than the time before.

"One night last year he was more violent than he'd ever been. He was drunk, of course, and they quarreled about me, as usual. I hate to say this about my own mother but she was jealous that he didn't look at her like he did at me. It never mattered to her that all I wanted was for him not to look at me at all, ever."

Jade stopped but gestured with her hand, "Back off," when we wanted to surround her. We stayed still and quiet until she continued.

"That night, she locked me in my room and hid the key. Once the argument started I could hear her screaming and these like thuds and grunts . . . for such a long, long time. Then suddenly total silence. That scared me worse than the awful sounds they'd been making.

"When I heard the front door slam I tried to get to her but the lock held no matter how much I pounded. There was no window or any way out. I dialed 911, again. It took them forever to come but a kind operator stayed on the phone with me. That was the third operator. The first two times I called while it was still happening all they'd said was that they would send someone when they could."

We could see Jade wasn't with us anymore but back trapped in her room, desperate. We waited until she spoke again.

"When the sirens finally pulled up I heard the front door battered down. Then more sirens and ambulance people shouting at each other. Although I couldn't see her, I could tell my mother was hurt real bad. They were making preparations to take her away when the 911 operator must have radioed them not to forget me. Somebody broke the lock to my room to let me out."

A moan took Jade's voice away. "Are you sure—" Piper started to ask.

Jade insisted, "No, I have to tell all of it." She looked at us then as if she was trying to remind herself she was safe with friends who loved her.

"I rode in the ambulance with my mother. She was unconscious. Later I found out she was in a coma. The EMTs were urgently doing all these things with machines. One of them told me it was to 'keep her stable.' After I'd been waiting in the ER for hours someone thought to call my aunt who came and got me."

Jade sighed then as if the memory of her aunt's comfort strengthened her.

"For a long time, they didn't think my mother would survive. I stayed with my aunt and I know that it's awful to say but I was really happy there. Not that I wanted my mother to die but it was such a relief to be . . . anyway, that ended.

"When they still thought my mother would die, my stepfather's lawyer convinced him to plead guilty to first degree assault. The way it was later explained to me, it was a defense tactic to try to avoid murder charges if she died. When the judge gave him a long sentence anyway, my stepfather was furious. I was there in the courtroom when it happened. My stepfather screamed at me that this was all my fault and I'd be sorry—"

"—No!" Piper blurted out but then covered her mouth so that Jade would continue.

"After my mother recovered—well she recovered enough to survive—my stepfather was angrier than ever as if she'd tricked him by not dying. What they told me later was that he tried to hire someone to kill the judge and the prosecutor and me. The inmate that was supposed to be the go-between reported my stepfather to the authorities. That's when Detective Ed was brought in and they set up a whole sting operation. They got my stepfather on tape trying to hire an undercover officer to torture us first and then kill us. My stepfather was convicted of such serious crimes that Ed promised me he would 'never see the stars at night' ever again.

"Still, there's always suspicions that my stepfather will try again. The judge and the prosecutor have enough influence that they secured all these lifetime protections for themselves. Detective Ed got really angry and demanded that if they got protected, I should too. Ed promised me the judge and prosecutor would be too embarrassed to oppose me having what they had. He must have been right.

"They installed this little icon on my phone that goes directly to the emergency protection system. It automatically transmits anything I've been recording at the time the signal gets activated. When Lance lunged at me I guess I hit the icon without knowing it. If it hadn't been for you—"

Jade turned to me then but I made a gesture to include everyone: "We saved each other and ourselves, like we're supposed to."

"Yes," Jade said sadly, "that's the way it's *supposed* to be.

"My mother recovered enough to go home but her body is . . . damaged. There are a lot of tasks she can't do for herself. They asked me if I was willing to take care of her. I agreed to move home although I knew I'd miss my aunt like crazy. That was my biggest mistake.

"As soon as we were alone my mother told me she hated me. My stepfather being in prison, she told me that's all my fault. No one will ever love me because I am bad deep inside. She reminds me every day."

When Jade got to that part we couldn't stay silent but she insisted on finishing.

"She lets me go to school and then here to study. She let me attend the hearing because she was afraid not to. Mostly though, my house is like a prison. I go home and I have to touch her body to do all these things she can't do for herself. She needs a nurse, really, but she would rather humiliate me by making me clean her and clean up after her—

"If it wasn't for Lilly-Belle, I would never escape it. I told my mother I had to do community service walking shelter dogs. She never even asked what I had to do community service *for*. Lilly-Belle, the little bit of time I'm with her, I feel like I'm a good person. But then I go home and my mother reminds me I'm not and never will be—"

"—No. Stop." Sunny had listened as long as she could. "You know it's a lie, Jade. You know it's always been a lie—"

"—Anybody Jade, anybody decent could never hate you for rescuing them—" Piper interrupted, but Sunny wasn't done.

"—Both of you, they *lied* and you let it tunnel in. Because somehow it was less hurtful than seeing the truth that the people who were supposed to love you could be so vile. It's like that kid calling *himself* 'Squeaky.' You let the lies have power. Now you have to—"

"—walk your own path, not the road *anyone* else paved for you," Tia went first, each of us saying it the way we needed to.

"—hear your own music." Rae-Rae.

"—bow to the self within." Dareen.

"—be my own mirror." Piper.

"—remember I am my true father's child." Jade.

"But no matter how right that all is"—I couldn't stay silent any longer—"Jade, you don't have to live like that! We'll talk to my lawyer. She'll get the courts to send you back to your aunt." The words spilled out because I was angry. Now I had to see it true.

My friends shut me up long enough to make sure Piper and Jade both knew in their hearts what we knew about them. And then because we were full up on emotions, the conversation turned practical.

Jade was worried she didn't have money to pay for a lawyer. That one was easy. I repeated what Ms. Horne had told me: "Children in this state are entitled to their own lawyers in abuse and neglect cases. The court appoints the lawyer and the government pays for it. But that's not the case everywhere. In some horrible states, children don't have those rights . . . only those who abuse them do." Ms. Horne had been so angry about those other states that her words had made a permanent impression.

Once we got back to the topic of whether to contact my lawyer, the other crisis we'd been keeping at bay resurfaced. On any other day, it would have been front and foremost. We were supposed to meet Ms. Horne tonight for news about Beemer. *Beemer!* I texted and we set it up to go to her offices early.

44

The afternoon had been too full. We decided we needed to take the long walk over to Ms. Horne's instead of a bus.

We were so subdued Rae-Rae couldn't put up with us. She announced it was the perfect time to sing great breakup songs. "Only way to truly get rid of demons," Rae-Rae promised. "Bob Dylan, he's the best of the bitter," she laughed. "Who could top 'You just kind of wasted my precious time'? Or how about Little Richard: 'You said you love me, but you can't come in'? I love that Theresa Brewer claimed 'Gonna Get Along Without You Now' for women but her way is still too soft.

"No, no, no! You know what we should do?" Rae-Rae didn't wait for an answer: "We should rewrite our own. There are songs that belong to all of us. It's called 'public domain.' You know what's my favorite of them? 'Who's Sorry Now.' Poor Connie Francis, her version is beautiful but she always sounds shattered. We need a *victorious* version."

"I'm too tired for victorious, Rae-Rae." It could have been any one of us who said that but, unexpectedly, it was Sunny.

"Just try it, OK? I'll start with Piper. 'Right to the end, before all my friends, I tried to warn you somehow—' "

Tia backed her: "—Who's had their day? Who's gonna pay?—"

Sunny and Dareen and I joined in: "—I know that you're sorry now."

Rae-Rae started another chorus: "Who's sorry now, who's sad and small?—"

Piper added tentatively: "You tried to hurt me that's all—"

Jade sang in a small but strong voice, "—I'm on my own, but I'm not alone—"

Rae-Rae finished for her, "—Who's sad and who's sorry now?"

Then we all did bits and pieces and created a third chorus:

"Who's happy now, who's proud and tall?

Whose heart's not aching or breaking at all?

We have this song to prove you were wrong.

We're glad that you're sorry now."

We sang it again all the way through until we felt it in our hearts. Rae-Rae got us home.

45

As soon as we got to my lawyer's office, Piper made an appointment to get a stalking order, looking serious but not grim. While Jade consulted Ms. Horne about moving to her aunt's, Piper gave Ethan and Hoke an edited version of Lance's arrest, leaving out Jade's secrets. Rae-Rae summed it up: "We took him *down!*"

Our friends were proud of us.

Tia couldn't let it go at that. She told Ethan, "When you first started training us, the exercise felt . . . inelegant. No matter what I did, I couldn't lose myself in its rhythm. I trusted you, not the exercise. Now I understand how right a choice that was."

Dareen joined in: "For me, the exercise did not feel enough like combat. I don't think I understood the concept of containment until you taught it to us. I will be forever grateful."

Piper was simpler: "If you hadn't picked the right technique and taught it to us perfectly, Jade and all of us, Lance would have hurt us like he'd meant to."

I added the part that was most important to me: "The day you sat in the studio deciding what we needed to learn, you couldn't have picked better than to teach us that we are our strongest fighting together."

While we were talking to Ethan, as right as it felt, a piece of my mind was preoccupied. Hoke put it into words: "Does anyone know why we're here?"

No one did. "I figure it has to be something about the school board but we got the same text you did," I answered him.

"No matter how much I try not to think about it," Sunny said quietly, "the more time it takes, the more it looks as if they're not going to do anything about Beemer. I keep telling myself to be proud of us anyway."

"We've stood up to worse," Rae-Rae added. I think maybe that's *her* mantra.

"No information is *no* information," corrected Tia.

"I'm done being scared," Piper smiled wryly, "but I have to admit my heart starts pounding thinking about what the board will decide."

Right when we were all agreeing, Mac the intern walked in looking infinitely pleased with himself. It exasperated but didn't surprise us that he wouldn't tell us anything.

Jade returned to the conference room more like the friend I remembered than she'd seemed in a long time. The first words out of her mouth though, were "You won't believe this!"

Ms. Horne—I hadn't even seen her enter—picked up a remote and aimed it. The intro to the 6:00 news popped into life on a large screen. "BREAKING NEWS," it flashed. The headline teaser came a moment later.

"LOCAL ADAMS CITY HIGH SCHOOL TEACHER ARRESTED ON CHARGES OF LURING, ATTEMPTED KIDNAPPING FOR SEXUAL PURPOSES, ONLINE SOLICITATION OF A MINOR, MORE."

The buzz around me was more sounds than words. None of us wanted to miss the actual coverage to ask questions. Despite it being the lead story, we had to sit through the other headlines and the commercial break before, as the announcer's voice returned, a mugshot filled the screen. *Beemer!*

"Adams High School Social Sciences teacher Frederick Beemer has been arrested on multiple charges for attempting to induce a fourteen-year-old girl into acts of perversion."

They showed a video clip of Beemer being perp-walked into a police station.

"According to the arrest warrant, the Adams County District Attorney's Child Exploitation Task Force received an informant's tip on their hotline two weeks ago. The tip, from a concerned family member, identified an autistic fourteen-year-old girl as the target of sexual advances by an older sibling's teacher.

"An undercover police officer, posing as the fourteen-year-old and using her phone, began texting with Frederick Beemer who believed he was talking to the girl. Beemer's texts included sexually explicit words and photos. Beemer was arrested when he arrived at the hotel where he had arranged to 'consummate' his relationship with the child before they left the state together to 'live as man and wife.'

"At no time during the investigation was the child at actual risk. It is nevertheless the policy of this news station not to name the victims of sexual assault.

"At the time of the investigation, Frederick Beemer was also the subject of an unrelated hearing by the Adams County District School Board concerning other alleged misconduct. At the request of the District Attorney's Office, the school board delayed its announcement of his termination for cause until after the teacher's arrest. The school board chairman requested that all news coverage of what he called this 'shameful incident' include the school board's reassurance that despite their principal being placed on administrative leave, classes at Adams City High School will resume as normal and counselors will be available for students.

"The Adams County District Attorney has set up a hotline for anyone with information or further complaints.

"Frederick Beemer's arraignment is scheduled for tomorrow morning in Adams County District Court, Part B."

Mac snorted. "I guess they're hoping no one will notice they axed The Tsar."

"Give them time to ask questions, Mac," Ms. Horne admonished as she hit mute.

We had a million we were almost too excited to ask.

Ethan went first: "What does termination mean?"

"Perfect question, Ethan," my lawyer praised him. "In this case, termination means a complete victory." We had to cheer, even though we wanted to hear the rest. "Frederick Beemer is fired permanently. He wasn't even vested so he has no pension or other rights. The board has also referred a complaint to the state to have his teaching license revoked."

After a round of clapping and "woo-hoos" my Hoke asked the logical next question: "Is it true that the school board had already decided to fire Beemer?"

"We will probably never know for certain but I doubt all of them had agreed," Ms. Horne answered carefully. "From what I heard, they believed our witnesses but they were still debating what to do at the point when they were first contacted by the DA's office. The loyalists argued additional training—"

"—As if!" Mac sneered.

"—was sufficient." Ms. Horne didn't bother to acknowledge her intern this time. "The cowards were worried about the school district's liability if they kept Beemer on after knowing that one student went mute and another nearly died. The wafflers wanted a short suspension and probation, but worried about pressure from the public after that editorial in *The Herald*. A few of the school board members, led by Colton Bridgeway, wanted to get rid of Beemer for all the right reasons. Once the board learned about the criminal investigation, they all wanted to vote immediately to be on record ahead of the charges. The investigators made them wait with the announcement until the undercover cop could lock down the proof of the crimes."

"Do you think the school board will listen better next time?" Dareen wanted to know.

"Dareen, yes. They learned a good lesson. Bridgeway used this fiasco to convince them that the only way to prevent things from getting this out of hand again is for them to adopt that policy he's wanted all along. Any teacher accused of bullying will be offered the option to sign a contract not to engage in that behavior in the future and acknowledge that the conduct is in fact bullying. At the very least it identifies problem teachers much earlier."

"Ms. Horne . . ." I hesitated.

My lawyer filled the gap by gently correcting me: "You can call me Naomi again, now that the hearing is over."

"If we'd waited ..."

"Anna, are you worried all our hard work was for nothing? I don't believe that. I think without the pressure we created Beemer would have gone on with his foul business as usual forever."

"I'm going to explode if I don't ask," Rae-Rae all but interrupted. "The Tsar is really gone? Why? I mean, not that I mind!"

Mac had been waiting on the edge of his seat. "Years of complaints about Beemer making sexual advances toward students. The Tsar's been covering for him all this time. Personally, I think the cops suspect The Tsar of more than what they know now—"

"—There may be more crimes," Ms. Horne stepped on whatever speculation Mac was about to share, "but what they know already is more than enough for the school board to want to distance itself from The Tsar. Right now he's on 'administrative leave.' The police have information about some online communications between Beemer and The Tsar." She cut her eyes appreciatively toward Hoke. *He never told me!* "My guess is that the board will wait until the criminal investigation is over before they decide what to do."

While the conversation continued around her, Rae-Rae took some drawing supplies out of her backpack.

"I'm not sure I understand what you meant that pressure made Beemer do what he did," I returned to my first question.

"No. Beemer did what he did because he is evil. Pressure didn't make him a rapist. It made him careless and rushed, more easily tricked. I suspect when you kept mentioning girls on the stand, Anna—"

"—That just popped out—"

"—he thought we knew more than what was in the OBaaT complaint. As far as we can tell this is the first time he's tried to get a girl to leave the state with him. He must have felt it was all catching up with him. He started making strategic mistakes. There's online evidence"—she glanced at Hoke again—"he emptied his bank accounts and when he was arrested he couldn't explain away why he was carrying so much cash just to meet someone. He hadn't planned. If he'd soothed over the older sister's feelings, for example, she might not have turned him in to the police."

"It was Berry!" Jade gasped. "She was jealous Beemer wanted her younger sister, not her!"

"I know Berry threatened you, Anna, and she tried to undermine you all. Maybe this is too much to ask . . . but I hope at some point you can find some sympathy in your hearts for any child so desperate for love they are willing to trade their bodies for the pretend version." We might have felt guilty then but Mac brought us back to the truth we knew.

"That Berry is a piece of work," he countered.

"I'm not denying that," his boss answered.

"Honestly, right now I don't care about Berry," Piper brought us back. "Just think about it. Did you ever dream we could take down this many bullies?! In one day?!" A giggle escaped from deep inside her.

"Yeah," Rae-Rae chimed in. "The only mistake we made is calling it OBaaT. One bully at a time—for us that'd be a vacation!"

"Do you remember what the mother of that boy with diabetes said to us? She told us her son asked her to testify because he wanted to go to school with kids like us." Dareen summed it up: "Now he can." Maybe because she understands combat better than the rest of us, she understands victory better too.

Rae-Rae held up the sign she'd been working on, graffiti-bold letters on a deep-purple background: "YSI, WFI."

We looked her the question.

"You Start It, We Finish It," Rae-Rae shouted.

"What happens next?" Tia asked, still laughing.

"You give us a poem," Sunny suggested.

Tia grew thoughtful, then lighter, then offered:

> Inside from a sharp cold night
> soup simmering on the stove
> steam wisps rising.

It rained the morning of the Rescues Rule! Festival but by 10:00 it was clear enough to set up and by noon it was exactly the kind of sunshiny day we'd been hoping for.

Sunny and Ethan organized a booth selling about a million homemade dog biscuits. They even persuaded the squirrel lady to sit with them. No squirrels though, or peanuts to lure them. Mamie explained, "Squirrels are just too smart for dogs and we didn't want to depress the canines."

Behind them, Sunny and Ethan had filled a huge bucket with all the broken bits and pieces of treats. About the tenth time I'd circled around to replenish my supply, leash attached to the latest tail-wagging creature wearing an ADOPT LOVE vest, I heard Rae-Rae squeal, "Charity! I can't believe you made it!"

Dogs just get it about affection. When Charity grabbed me in a hug bigger than she was, the furball I was walking joined in so exuberantly he sent the three of us rolling onto the grass. If Ethan hadn't thought to rescue the bits and pieces bucket, we probably would have had a mutt-riot.

We only enjoyed but a minute of laughter though before Charity arranged her sketching materials and an easel, promising a free line portrait of any dog adopted that day. It must have taken all her self-discipline to broad-stroke the drawings instead of her usual meticulous intricacies. She was instantly surrounded and I had to whisper a promise to get back to her when things quieted down.

I scooped up another handful of treats before the furball and I continued our walk, stopping by Dareen's so-called enclosure. Greene Street had rescued a litter of dachshunds now ready for adoption. Early this morning Dareen's grandmother had driven a large square of stakes into the ground as fence posts. Dareen and her mother had spent hours carefully constructing a mesh-screened puppy playground. If you only considered the visual, it was a design marvel. That is if you completely forgot the tunneling ability of dachshunds. It took the puppies a maximum of 90 seconds of human inattention to dig under the fence and squirt off in various directions, with Dareen chasing madly behind.

Finally Jade and her aunt took pity on Dareen and sat outside the enclosure snatching up the little runaways one by one. Jade kept laughing every time one of the squirmies wound up in her hands. Living with her aunt, she'd started to remember how to be happy.

That dachshund strategy would have worked except that Lilly-Belle arrived with both the assisted living resident and her attendant in tow. They wanted to brag to Jade that Lilly-Belle was now the star attraction at the facility. The woman gloated, "I've never had this much company in my whole life!"

As soon as Jade was distracted warming in that victory, one of the puppies made another run for it. Before the humans could make fools of themselves again, Lilly-Belle calmly and delicately scooped up the puppy in her jaws by the scruff of its neck and deposited it back in Dareen's hands. I swear Lilly-Belle grinned at me. And that she looked years younger. It made me happy seeing Jade and Lilly-Belle together. They needed each other less now but they loved each other exactly as much.

Dareen may have misplaced her dignity—or had it stolen by dachshund puppies—but Tia managed to look centered and perfectly postured even elbow-deep in water and wet fur at the dog wash she was working. She waved a sudsy hand at me and pointed with her eyebrows raised at Charity in the distance still surrounded by newly adopted joy.

I loved it that so many pits in all their muttly variations were in the line waiting to be immortalized on paper. Maybe folks were finally starting to understand. I spotted my favorite pair, the honey-colored pit bull and her scary-looking goofus mate-for-life. A sweet family, who'd recently had to let go of both their pits within a week of each other, had no problem with the idea that these two came as an indivisible unmatched set.

Rocky showed up with a family in tow as exuberant as he was. The Rottweiler mix gave me and my current walking dog a drive-by burst of good cheer before continuing on his mission to celebrate with each creature at the festival.

Someone stopped me then to ask about the friendly faced big mutt I was walking. I liked the dog a lot but I'd only just met him. I escorted them over to the volunteer who'd worked with him the most. On my way back, I rescued a newbie volunteer trying to walk Polar Bear. *What was she thinking!* He looked quite fetching in his huge ADOPT LOVE vest but his obedience was not a whole lot improved. I knew Polar Bear had a soft spot in his heart for Jade, but adding him to the mix with Lilly-Belle and the tiny dachshund felons didn't seem like a good idea. What had Rae-Rae said so beautifully about Polar Bear belonging with Piper?

"Polar Bear, I've got the girl for you. The one you've been waiting for. But you have to be your absolute best so she realizes it, OK?" Usually I avoid making promises to the dogs, especially Polar Bear who always seems like he might understand.

We angled toward Hoke where he was helping an agility trainer set up an entire portable course complete with weave poles, jumps, a teeter-totter, tunnels, and ramps. The geometry of it drew Hoke in. The trainer had demo dogs that had been adopted out of Greene Street. The first few were fine jumping and running and burrowing from obstacle to obstacle with exuberant abandon with their found families cheering them on. But then the trainer went too far trying to prove versatility. He had Hoke lower all the jumps until they were only a couple of inches off the ground. I expected he would demonstrate some small dogs but instead, he brought out a basset hound who had the crowd chuckling before she even entered the track.

"It's like you can hear tuba music playing in the background," Rae-Rae told me. I hadn't heard her come up beside me and Polar Bear. To her credit, the basset moved ever so slow but steady, ears dragging perilously close to the ground, through obstacles I hadn't thought she could manage—*basset on a teeter-totter!*—until she got to the jumps . . . and screeched on the brakes.

The crowd started clapping, which pleased the basset to no end but the trainer, not so much. He tried again to encourage the dog, who wasn't having any. You could just see the stalled dog announcing emphatically, "We bassets do not jump." Her expression made Rae-Rae and I laugh so hard I almost fell down again. I suspect that's what brought Piper—with her dad trailing her—over to all of us from behind the track. Like they were magnetized by our good humor.

"Oh how gorgeous he is!" Piper admired Polar Bear. I could see the Great Pyr's chest expanding. No small feat. "Can I pat him?" Polar Bear answered for me, sighing blissfully into her affection.

"Oh girl, it's so you!" Rae-Rae imitated idiots who consider a dog a fashion accessory. Only funny because we all knew Piper hated that concept even more than Rae-Rae did. Piper and Polar Bear being made for each other had nothing to do with how beautiful they both were. Rae-Rae summed it up: "They have the same music."

Piper hunched down halfway, meeting the big white dog's gaze more or less eye to eye. "What do you think, Polar Bear?" she asked him only a split second before—*who* couldn't *see this coming*—he tongue-washed her entire face in one swipe. They both giggled in delight.

"You know, Piper," her father said thoughtfully. "I've been thinking you should get a dog."

"I'm safe now, Dad," Piper reassured him.

"I know, I know. But I'd still rest easier ..."

Polar Bear decided humans were too slow on the uptake. While the agility trainer coaxed the reluctant basset back into the shade to the welcome arms of her bemused family, Polar Bear seized the opportunity to drag me around the entire agility course. A few steps into it and I realized he knew his way around the obstacles. I let him take the lead—as much as that was an actual choice. Because the jumps were set too low he kind of stepped over them without noticing, but the rest of his performance was flawless. I didn't even feel guilty that he was winning over Piper and her father under false pretenses. Let them find out his willfulness *after* they fall in love with him. Polar Bear is an ideal protection dog, I reminded myself. I knew he had them when Piper assured her father that her mother would accept Polar Bear's flaws during the weeks Piper lived there because he was gorgeous. They both knew her mother.

The trainer offered to teach Piper how to direct Polar Bear through the agility course: "He's a natural, and he's done this before." Spotting the potential, the trainer lectured Piper's father: "I throw in five free lessons with every Rescues Rule! adoption I have any part in. It's a great way for the two of them"—he nodded toward Piper and what already looked like *her* dog—"to learn to work together. And who knows, she may love it. I personally think agility is the most and healthiest fun a dog and human can have together."

I thought it was too much of a hard sell but I was wrong. When Piper's father started musing about helping with training I signaled one of the Greene Street staff to take this maybe-adoption to the next step. Predictably, Rae-Rae was less cautious. She ran off after announcing, "I have to go tell Charity about the great dog she's going to draw next. Maybe we'll do this one together, mixed media like. Polar Bear, we'll make you a rock star!"

Someone handed me the leash of a pit bull I'd never met before. The dog gave me a kind of imploring look until I crouched in front of her. Then she purposefully hooked her left paw over my wrist and insisted I rub her heart. As soon as I did, her ears turned pink with pleasure and she smiled with cartoon-dog squiggle lips. I knew immediately we were going to be great pals. While Piper and her dad were busy with Polar Bear, Hoke and I walked this new dog around Rescues Rule! only the three of us. It felt as far from lonely as I've ever been.

A note from the author

The Legislative Drafting Institute for Child Protection (LDICP.
org) takes requests from grassroots organizations to research
and write policies and laws to protect underage people from mistreatment. That's all they do—they don't take on individual cases.
The LDICP does not charge for its services but requires that the
organization doing the asking is committed to making the law
or policy a reality. Policies about school bullying by teachers and
professors would definitely fit the kinds of issues they work on.
Anyone can contact them at LDICPinfo@gmail.com but if you
mention OBaaT it will help them know the kind of policy change
you're looking to accomplish. First, though, you have to decide
this is your fight and then you have to put together a group of
friends and supporters who believe it is theirs too.